Ruthie ran down the stairs, curious to learn what the ruckus was about.

Standing in the foyer was Lucy, who had in her hand a new gown for the Winter Ball. "Let me run up and put it on!" she shouted.

Minutes later, Lucy came down the stairs like a princess descending the winding staircase of a castle. Her gown was long, red, and full, and her golden hair hung long and shiny across the top of it.

Lucy excitedly explained that her date, the *President of the Student Government*, was renting a limo for the ball. Not only that, they were double-dating with the coolest couple on campus! It would be the most romantic night of her life!

7th Heaven™

WINTER BALL

by *Amanda Christie*

An Original Novel

*Based on the hit TV series
created by Brenda Hampton*

Random House 🏠 New York

www.randomhouse.com/teens

Library of Congress Control Number: 2001094303
ISBN: 0-375-81430-2

Printed in the United States of America
First Edition
January 2002
10 9 8 7 6 5 4 3 2 1

RANDOM HOUSE and colophon are
registered trademarks of Random House, Inc.

7th Heaven.

WINTER BALL

ONE

Lucy woke up in a college dormitory for the first time in her life. Her suitcase sat in the middle of the floor, overflowing with clothes and collegiate books. She yawned, her eyes still closed to the morning sun.

Suddenly they opened.

I'm not at home anymore, am I?

Lucy sat upright in bed. She looked around the dorm room, which belonged to her friend Bethany, who was in Europe for the month on a study-abroad program. Last week at church when Lucy had told her she was considering living on campus next semester, Bethany had said, "Take my place while I'm away. Try it out, see if you like it."

A week later, everything had been cleared with the college, and now here she was, alone, in the dormitories—where everyone else had spent the previous semester making dorm friends. Lucy hated to admit it, but she already felt out of place and lonely.

Chin up, Lucy, this is supposed to be exciting!

She rolled out of bed and felt a rumble in her stomach. She was starving. Last night when all the other girls in the hall were cooking in the kitchen, Lucy had realized she hadn't brought anything to eat but a granola bar—and all the on-campus eateries had been closed. She needed to get to the cafeteria as quickly as possible.

She looked in the mirror and her face soured. How could she possibly cross campus looking this way? She grabbed a ponytail holder and pulled her hair back.

You look fine the way you are, she counseled herself. *Now go get some food from the cafeteria.*

Lucy pushed open her door and started off down the hallway, where posters, bumper stickers, and pictures were plastered across all the doors. The door across from her had posters of cool bands, and the door to the left was covered with pictures of modern dancers. And then there was the room at the end of the hall. Its door was covered with black-and-white photography, taken by the two talented roommates who lived inside.

Why did she suddenly feel so boring? How had she been so popular in high school but become utterly invisible in college? All the confidence and security she used to have was gone. She felt like a little seventh grader all over again. Like Mary Camden's dorky younger sister.

As Lucy reached for the exit door, she heard a stampede behind her. She turned around and saw a whole gang of girls running down the stairs, racing each other.

One girl yelled, "Loser buys breakfast!" The others burst out laughing as they ran right past Lucy. They busted through the door without even noticing her.

She caught the door before it closed

again, watching the girls continue their marathon through the quad. She sighed and walked out onto the grassy lawn. She looked up at the clouds, certain that it was about to rain.

Halfway to the cafeteria, a large drop of water landed smack-dab on the tip of Lucy's nose. And then another on her forehead. Lucy walked faster. She looked down at the sidewalk, which was quickly darkening with round gray spots.

"I don't even have a jacket," Lucy moaned out loud. "And I'm wearing white!"

She heard a bicycle as it whirred behind her. Seconds later, a cute upperclassman raced by. Lucy had noticed him before at a rally, and she felt her heart rate quicken.

"Nice stripes!" he yelled.

Lucy paled and looked down. She was wearing her red-striped underwear and it was showing through her wet pants. Could this morning get any worse?

The boy looked back and smiled, then raced off. Lucy's face turned bright red.

Great, now my face and my underwear match.

Lucy ducked into the nearest building and realized it was the science hall. She was grateful for one thing as she took refuge in the warm lobby: only science geeks would see her in her candy-cane clothing.

She picked up a science journal from the nearest table and held it across her backside as she inspected postings on the lobby corkboard.

Science fairs. Star Trek *conventions, lectures on laser technologies, blah, blah, blah . . .*

But then a poster caught her eye. A poster of a young man in a tuxedo dancing with a young woman in a beautiful red gown. It was a poster for the Winter Ball, the biggest formal event of the year. Lucy felt her sadness fade as romantic thoughts consumed her.

Imagine having a dress and a date like that!

Just then, Lucy felt a tap on her shoulder. She turned around and found herself standing face to face with a freckle-faced, redheaded girl. A girl wearing glasses so thick Lucy could barely make out the color of her eyes. It was

Tanya, a girl on her hall with whom Lucy shared a class.

"Think we'll *ever* find a date to the dance?" Tanya squeaked, her voice so soft Lucy had to lean in to hear her.

"What?" Lucy asked.

Tanya stood up straighter, as though preparing to deliver a monologue from a stage. "The dance!" Tanya projected loudly. "Think we'll find dates?"

Lucy shook her head and laughed. Tanya was undoubtedly a quirky girl. "Not at the rate I'm going. It's only two weeks away."

But then something else caught Lucy's eye. She moved closer to read the fine print on the poster.

Tanya peered over Lucy's shoulder, as though she had happened upon a conspiracy. "What's wrong?" Tanya whispered.

Lucy smiled, explaining as she read. "The Winter Ball is a fund-raiser for charities."

Tanya's brow furrowed in confusion. "And . . . ?"

Lucy turned to Tanya. "The student

council is looking for volunteers to help organize the dance."

Tanya still wasn't sure why this news had perked Lucy up so visibly. "So you're excited because you want some extra work? I can give you some computer code to write if you're that bored."

Lucy shook her head, still grinning. "If we get involved, we'll be helping raise money for charity *and* meeting people. *People who may not have dates.*"

Suddenly Tanya's confusion turned to clarity. She nodded, and Lucy noticed that her smile was vibrant and her teeth were as straight and white as an actor's in a toothpaste commercial. She wasn't an unattractive girl underneath those Coke-bottle glasses.

"And even if we don't find dates, we can still have fun," Lucy said, masking her real fear with nonchalance. What if she really *couldn't* find a date?

She shrugged off the insecurity and continued her thought. "Fund-raisers are great. I even know the perfect charity."

Tanya linked her arm in Lucy's. "Okay, *but* we're finding dates."

Lucy laughed as she looked outside. The rain was still pouring down. And Lucy was still hungry. Tanya seemed to read Lucy's thoughts.

"Who cares about your pants? Let's eat."

Tanya opened the door and pulled Lucy out into the rain. In seconds, they were squealing and running for the cafeteria.

But now they were armed with a plan. . . .

The front door of the Camden house was thrown open with the force of a tornado. The doorknob hit the wall with a *thud* and then bounced back against the fifth-grade girl who now stood in the doorway. But Ruthie Camden paid the door no mind.

She looked into the living room.

"Hey," she said to an empty room.

Where was her mother? Her brother Simon? Anyone to hear her good news?

Ruthie ran into the kitchen, her chunky heels clopping across the tile. In the last year, she'd sprouted a full four inches and was determined to catch up with her big sister Lucy in another year. Until then, the chunky shoes would have to do the trick.

"Hey!" she shouted again.

The twins, Sam and David, looked up from their kiddie chairs at the table.

"Where's Mom?"

The two boys threw diced-up sandwich pieces at one another and laughed.

"Lot of good you three-year-olds are!"

Ruthie spun around and ran up the stairs, banging the wall like a drum as she took the steps two at a time. She reached the landing and stopped.

"Mom! Simon! Anyone!"

Her mother, Mrs. Camden, rushed out of the twins' bedroom with two clean T-shirts in her hand. She rushed right past Ruthie, patting her head as she went.

"The twins!" she exclaimed, as though that explained everything. She started to rush downstairs when a loud screech forced her to stop.

"Waaaaiiiiiitttttttt!"

Mrs. Camden turned around and stared wide-eyed at her daughter, who was *not* the screeching type. Ruthie's frustration spilled into a wide smile when she saw the shocked response her screech had elicited.

"May I help you?" Mrs. Camden asked calmly.

"Mom!"

"Yes . . . ?"

"You're *so* not gonna believe this!"

Mrs. Camden nodded. "You do realize that you don't need the word *so* to give your exclamation emphasis, don't you?"

"Yes—"

"And you do know that it's grammatically incorrect to place this word before any word that's not an adjective or an adverb, right?"

"Mom!"

Mrs. Camden calmly nodded. "I'm listening."

But a new idea occurred to Ruthie and she held out her hand like a traffic director demanding that a car stop moving. "Wait."

Then she screeched again. *"Simon!"*

Mrs. Camden put her hands over her ears. "What is with that screech, Ruthie?"

Simon's annoyed head appeared from the bathroom doorway. "Who's screeching?"

Ruthie put her hands on her hips and smiled. "I am."

"Why?" her older brother asked.

"Because Justin Taylor invited me to the movies!"

Silence greeted Ruthie.

Ruthie greeted the silence with a scoff. How dare they not respond to such earth-shattering news?

Finally, Simon shrugged. "Who's Justin Taylor?"

Ruthie rolled her eyes. "You mean you've never heard of him? He's the most popular boy in the fifth grade."

Mrs. Camden raised her hand. "May I ask a question?"

Ruthie ignored her. "Me first. Can I borrow your diamond necklace?"

Simon burst out laughing. "Right!"

Ruthie glared at him. "Why not?"

Mrs. Camden looked at Ruthie. "Are Justin's parents planning to attend this 'date' of yours?"

The question itself was enough to force Ruthie to take a step back in horror. How could her mother even suggest such an awful thought?

Mrs. Camden patted Ruthie's head

again as she started back down the stairs.
"Then I'm sorry to say that the answer is
no. As for the diamond necklace, we can
talk about that in five or ten years."

Ruthie ran down after her mother, so
deflated that even her shoes couldn't save
her from the sinking realization that, in
the world's distorted eyes, she was still a
kid. But just as she was about to scream
for more attention, the phone rang. She
heard Simon pick it up.

"Ruthie!" he yelled with a pointed lilt
to his voice. "It's *Justin*!"

Ruthie froze in the kitchen, staring at
the phone in terror. How could she tell
Justin Taylor no? She glared at her
mother, who calmly explained, "You're a
fifth grader, Ruthie."

Ruthie closed her eyes and pondered
the potential ramifications of turning
Justin down. "What am I going to say?
That my mother's too lame to let me go
on a date?"

Mrs. Camden shrugged as she pulled
the new clean T-shirts over the twins'
heads. "Invite him here next weekend.
Have a Valentine's Day party."

Ruthie's jaw dropped to the floor. She

looked at her mother as though she had just been beamed down from an alien planet.

"Did you actually say the word *party*?"

Mrs. Camden smiled. "I've thrown a good party or two in my day."

Ruthie picked her jaw up off the floor, then reached for the phone. It was too good to be true!

TWO

On the morning of the student council's volunteer meeting, Lucy knocked on Tanya's door. When Tanya answered, Lucy was surprised to find that her hallmate was still dressed in her pajamas.

"Get dressed, girlfriend!" Lucy exclaimed.

Tanya shook her head and sighed. "I don't want to go."

Confused, Lucy stepped inside the room and closed the door. Once inside, she was amazed to see that the room was filled from wall to wall with science fiction posters, fantasy books, action figures, stuffed toys, and models of starships.

"I thought you were excited to find a date," Lucy said.

Tanya shrugged and jumped back into her bed, pulling the covers up around her freckled face. "I'm afraid of crowds," Tanya said. "They make me nervous."

"Then why did you say you'd come?" Lucy asked.

"Because it was Friday."

Lucy looked at her in confusion.

"Back then, the meeting was two whole days away. Now it's only two minutes away."

Lucy picked up a stuffed green alien from Tanya's desk and inspected the strange creature. She linked her finger through its long, skinny arm, then faced Tanya. "But you'll have me with you. Together we can fend off the ugly upperclassmen."

Tanya threw off her covers, stood up, and saluted Lucy as though she were a starship captain. "Together we can beat the Borg."

Lucy laughed. "The Borg?"

"*Hello.* From *Star Trek: The Next Generation* and *Voyager*."

Lucy rolled her eyes. "*Star Trek, Schmar Schmeck.* Just tell me you'll go."

Tanya dove back into bed like a spaceship docking in its port. "I don't think so."

Lucy crossed her arms, thinking. Then she smiled. "I'll watch *Star Trek* with you every Wednesday night for the rest of the school year."

Shocked, Tanya looked up through her thick glasses. "For the rest of the year?"

The deal was sealed.

Fifteen minutes later, Lucy and Tanya quietly entered the appointed lecture hall. They were late. Almost every seat in the place—over two hundred of them—was filled with the university's elected representatives, none of whom were freshmen.

"Are you *sure* we're allowed to attend?" Tanya whispered, looking around at the representatives, each of whom sat behind nameplates as if they were members of Congress.

Lucy shrugged. "The poster said they wanted volunteers to help with the ball. That's what we are, right?"

The two girls looked for open seats and

finally spotted two down in the very front of the hall. They looked at each other and rolled their eyes. Of course the seats would be up front, where everyone could watch the two newcomers enter.

They quietly made their way down the center aisle, but a young man's voice, echoing over a microphone system, stopped them.

"Are you here about the ball?"

Lucy and Tanya looked up at the stage in horror, knowing that everyone was looking at them. But the nightmare only worsened when Lucy realized that the young man standing behind the lectern was the guy on the bike—the one who had teased her about her underwear! He was smiling down at Lucy, his shiny brown hair accentuating the darkness of his eyes.

Lucy felt her face redden again, then coughed when Tanya's elbow ground into her side. Tanya was too terrified to speak.

"Uh . . . yes," Lucy sputtered.

The guy spun his gold watch around his wrist so that the face was looking up. He glanced quickly down at it, then placed his hand into his pocket.

"Excellent. You're just in time," he said with a grin. "I'm Kent, the student government president."

Lucy attempted to return the smile, but at the moment she almost got her mouth muscles working again, an auburn-haired girl standing near an adjacent doorway waved her hand at Kent. She had a long braid and penetrating blue eyes. She seemed irritated.

Kent nodded quickly at the girl but didn't meet her eyes. Instead, he looked down at Lucy and Tanya. "The officers are splitting off to meet with volunteers in the adjoining classroom."

He motioned toward the door where the girl had stood just seconds before. But now the girl was retreating into the room, and Lucy saw her drop angrily into a chair. In the seat next to her, a sandy-haired guy stood up. He walked into the doorway, smiled, and waved the two girls in.

"Follow Graham," Kent said, his voice calm. "He's our vice president."

Lucy and Tanya nodded and made their way back across the lecture hall, thankful to have an exit, as Kent continued the government meeting. Graham, who the girls both recognized from events on campus, welcomed the two and told them to choose their seats.

Lucy grabbed the closest two seats and motioned Tanya to sit beside her. The room was filled with volunteers. In the front of the room, a small group of people, who Lucy assumed were officers, sat behind a table. The girl with the braid was one of them. Her eyes were looking the two girls over. "Are you ASG members?" she asked.

Lucy was feeling more uncomfortable by the minute. "What's ASG?" she asked quietly.

The girl seemed annoyed that Lucy didn't know what the letters stood for. "Associated Student Government," she coolly responded.

Lucy's face reddened again. "Oh . . . no. We saw a flyer and were hoping to volunteer," she said.

The girl looked at Graham, her frustration rising. "I thought the volunteers were supposed to be ASG members?"

Graham shrugged. "The poster didn't stipulate that."

The girl rolled her eyes. "It was implied. The ball is an ASG-sponsored event."

Lucy exchanged embarrassed looks with Tanya. "Maybe we should go," she whispered. But before the two could stand up, the girl addressed them again.

"Are you freshmen?" the girl asked.

Lucy and Tanya both nodded.

The girl shook her head. "This is a definite no. There are no freshmen allowed on the ball committee. This is the biggest event of the year."

Graham shrugged his shoulders, and the girl threw up her hands.

"I'm so frustrated by the lack of organization around here," she exclaimed. "There are rules, and we should all know them and follow them. Especially those of us at the top."

Just then, Kent walked into the room.

"Let's get this meeting started!" he said.

Lucy and Tanya stood up to go, but Kent turned to look at them. "Where do *you* two think you're going?"

The girl stood up and glowered at Kent. "They're not ASG members, Kent."

Kent looked at her, his face expressionless. "And . . . ?"

"And they're freshmen."

Kent shrugged and sat down at the table's center seat. "Volunteers are volunteers. We're lucky to have them. Now let's get started." He opened his notebook and pulled a pen from his pocket. "First and foremost, let's learn our new committee members' names."

He looked straight at Lucy, his dark brown eyes lively and penetrating. Lucy felt her palms begin to sweat.

What is it about that look?

"Uh . . . I'm Lucy," she said.

"And do you have a last name, Lucy?"

"Camden."

Kent grinned warmly. "Welcome."

"Thanks," Lucy sputtered, her eyes dropping to the desk before her. Kent turned his gaze to Tanya.

"And our other unlucky inductee would be?"

Tanya closed her eyes and spat out the words. "Tanya Berringer."

Kent smiled. "We're extremely glad to have you." He motioned to his officer. "I know you've met Graham. Our secretary is Rachel."

A plastic smile spread across Rachel's face. She nodded at Lucy and Tanya. "I'm sorry to be less enthusiastic than Kent about newcomers, but we've already got a lot of hands in the pot, if you know what I mean, and I don't want to ruin the dish." She smiled again. "But I'm sure that won't happen."

Kent introduced the other officers, then explained that the committee would be separated into three subcommittees. The first committee was the charity committee. He asked if there was anyone in the room that had a charity they felt passionate about. Lucy raised her hand and was certain that she felt Rachel bristle.

Why doesn't this girl like me?

But Lucy ignored the feeling and stood up. As soon as she began talking about the charity she loved, the words suddenly came to her with ease. For a minute, she felt like the old Lucy again.

"I'm an active member of Habitat for Humanity, and the local chapter could really use some financial help. They build homes for poor families, but they're low on funds this year. Maybe we could funnel some of the funds that we raise to them?"

Kent nodded, impressed. "I say we put Lucy on the charity committee."

The other officers, with the exception of Rachel, nodded.

Lucy suddenly remembered Tanya. "Can Tanya join the committee as well?"

Kent looked at the others. "Anyone opposed?"

There were no hands or nods. Rachel, however, did have something to say.

"We meet every morning at seven A.M. sharp. You can't be late."

Lucy looked at Tanya, who nodded. Lucy looked back at Rachel and gave her the most sincere, warm smile she could muster. If she had to work with this girl to get money to Habitat, she might as well try to be nice. "We'll be there!"

After the meeting, Lucy and Tanya made their way outside, glad to finally be out of the intimidating atmosphere. But beneath Lucy's anxiety was an incredible sense of accomplishment—she had made her way onto an ASG committee without being a member *or* an upperclassman.

Just then, Tanya grabbed Lucy's arm.

"I'm going to die," Tanya whispered.

Lucy looked at her, alarmed. "Why?"

Tanya motioned toward the sidewalk, where Graham was making his way out to his car. "He's so smart! I heard him speak on a panel in our department."

Lucy looked at Tanya. "You have a crush on him, don't you?"

Tanya grinned, nodding. "Like we'd ever have a chance with those two."

"*Two?*"

Tanya rolled her eyes. "Your face turned pomegranate red every time Kent spoke."

Lucy laughed and slipped her arm through Tanya's. "You're right—we don't have a chance."

Back at the Camdens', Ruthie was lugging Simon's stereo down the stairs to the living room. She stopped on the central landing, put the stereo on the ground, and sat down. She unbuckled her shoes and took them off.

Oh, the price of being stylish.

Now well balanced, Ruthie stood back up and hoisted the stereo into her little arms. She carefully started back down the steps, sweat forming on her intent brow.

When Ruthie reached the living room, she placed the stereo on top of the TV.

Perfect.

She took a step back, examining the configuration from afar as she pondered the meaning of her Valentine's Day bash. Without question, it was the most important night of her life. It would skyrocket her already top-notch reputation into the stratosphere. She would go down in the annals of fifth-grade history as the hippest hostess ever to grace the halls of her academy.

My party will rock Glenoak like it's never been rocked before.

As she reached out to set the volume dial to ten, Mrs. Camden walked into the room with a stack of folded towels. "What's with the stereo?"

Ruthie put one hand on the stereo bass control and the other on the treble. "Ever heard of dancing?"

Mrs. Camden took Ruthie's bass hand and stretched it out in front of her. Then she peeled Ruthie's other hand from the treble. Mrs. Camden gently placed the towels in Ruthie's arms. "Have you ever heard of completing your chores before dinner?"

Ruthie rolled her eyes and started out the door with the towels. "Ever heard of moving the furniture so your daughter can have a dance floor?"

Mrs. Camden followed Ruthie. "You've got your own muscles."

Ruthie kept walking. "Yeah, but I can't move the *couch*."

"You can dance around it. I've seen you."

Ruthie sighed audibly. "Yeah, but my friends can't."

Suddenly Mrs. Camden stopped walking. "Wait. Are we talking about your party?"

Ruthie opened the kitchen drawers and put the small towels inside them. "Duh."

Mrs. Camden shook her head. "First off, you're acting very haughty for a fifth grader, so I would watch my tone if I were you. And second, there will be no dancing at your party."

With the kitchen drawers extended in midair, Ruthie froze, staring at her mother in disbelief. "You're kidding, right?"

Mrs. Camden's expression remained unchanged. "You're eleven, Ruthie. You're not even a teenager."

Her words cut like a knife into Ruthie's heart. "I'm less than two years away," Ruthie argued.

"I'm happy to help you move the stereo back to Simon's room."

Ruthie looked at her mother—so now she'd help move things, huh? Ruthie grabbed a shaker of salt and handed it to her mother.

"What's this?" Mrs. Camden asked.

"It's salt for you to throw into my wound."

Mrs. Camden attempted to hide the smile that was creeping up around the edges of her mouth. But Ruthie was no dummy. She spotted the half-smile and spun around to head upstairs. Being eleven was more difficult than Ruthie had ever imagined. Suddenly all the fights that Simon, Lucy, and Mary once had with her parents made perfect sense.

"How can I have a party if there's no dancing?" she asked over her shoulder.

Mrs. Camden shrugged. "Have a movie-watching party."

Hmm. Not a horrible idea.

Ruthie sat down on a step and crossed her arms. "I'll settle for the compromise if we can watch the movie in the dark while you're in the backyard with Dad."

Mrs. Camden laughed out loud. "Then there's no compromise."

Ruthie slumped on the step. She needed a new plan of action before her popularity rating went from 9.5 to zero. And then she had an idea: she could call Lexie, who was a perfect ten, for some party advice.

THREE

Lucy had never been so excited to be up at seven A.M. She blew her hair dry and was delighted to find that it looked better than it had in months. In fact, it looked so good that Lucy didn't even think she needed makeup. She slipped on a baby-blue sweater and looked in the mirror.

Was I really so plain just three days ago? How could that be? I look pretty good now!

As Lucy and Tanya walked across campus, there was only one thing that was killing Lucy's buzz: What if Kent wasn't on her committee? What if she got stuck working with just Rachel?

A few minutes later, Lucy and Tanya

walked into the meeting room, where the chairs had been arranged in a large circle. Tanya nudged Lucy when she saw Graham sitting in a chair. Lucy smiled, happy for her friend. But then her heart sank when she realized that Kent wasn't in the room—but Rachel was.

Almost two weeks with this girl could do me in.

But instead of scowling at Lucy, Rachel smiled and patted the seat next to her. Confused, Lucy returned the smile and sat down. Rachel immediately leaned over and whispered, "Don't take yesterday personally."

Lucy looked at her, surprised. "I . . . I guess I did."

Rachel shook her head. "I'm a little territorial about the ball. I didn't know you, so it threw me off. I've been working on this event since last year, and now that it's almost here, suddenly Graham and Kent have jumped in and started making all the decisions. It's like handing your baby over to strangers."

Lucy nodded, realizing that what Rachel said made a lot of sense.

Lucy felt the tension in her whole

body relax. "Thanks for telling me. To be honest, I was a little freaked out."

Rachel laughed and patted Lucy's arm warmly. "Trust me, my bark is much worse than my bite."

Just then, Kent came running in. Lucy looked at Rachel, confused. "Are all the officers on this committee?"

Rachel nodded. "We're on all of them." Then Rachel noticed a glimmer in Lucy's eye. She raised an eyebrow. "Why? You have a crush on Kent?" she whispered.

Lucy felt her face get hot again. She shook her head. "No, I just thought you each had your own committee."

Rachel laughed. "I wish it were that easy. This is a big event for the university. There's no room for error."

Lucy nodded as Kent took a seat across from her. She tried not to look at him, but in the quick glance she allowed herself, she was struck by how handsome he was—not to mention how impeccably dressed. He could have walked straight out of a Manhattan attorney's office.

Suddenly Lucy felt his eyes on her. She looked up and he smiled at her. Then he glanced around to make sure no one else was looking. They weren't. He held up his notebook and Lucy read the words:

Sorry about the "nice stripes" joke.

Lucy smiled and looked at her desk, embarrassed that he'd brought it up. But then she noticed him flipping a page on his notebook. When she looked up again, another page was filled with words:

On the day I ran for ASG president, I sat down in a tray of Hershey's syrup. I was wearing white. It was an interesting speech, to say the least. But I won my presidential position in spite of Hershey's syrup.

Lucy laughed and Kent put his notebook away, suddenly all business again. He stood up and looked at the others, who were all talking among themselves.

"Shall we begin?"

The room fell quiet, and Kent looked at Graham.

"Graham has a strategic and financial

presentation to give, so take it away, Graham."

Lucy attempted to concentrate on the business at hand. But how could she concentrate when Kent was sitting right across from her? And what was she to make of his notes? Was he flirting with her, or was he just a nice guy? Maybe he flirted with everybody?

Focus on the meeting, Lucy.

Lucy looked at Graham, who was talking about money. He flipped his tie over his shoulder as he went to the chalkboard. He drew a diagram and wrote several figures in two columns.

"We're going to *double* the amount of money that last year's ball raised," he said, scribbling furiously, his mind racing quickly through figures and statistics. Lucy looked at Tanya, whose eyes were glazed over as she watched him. Tanya was right. Graham was certainly smart.

"Now," Graham said, and turned away from the chalkboard. "Here is how I propose we double our profits: I've found a caterer who will give us an excellent price on alcohol. They'll set up the bar, provide the booze, and we'll get fifty percent of their profit."

Did he say booze?

Suddenly Lucy forgot about Kent, her mind zeroing in on Graham's words.

Did he say we'd be selling alcohol at a school dance? That's impossible! What if somebody drove home drunk? What if minors were able to drink? What if . . .

Lucy wanted to speak out but immediately censored herself. She wasn't a senior at Kennedy High anymore, she was a freshman in college. An unknown freshman surrounded by upperclassmen. What if everyone thought she was a dork for even being concerned about having alcohol at a college dance?

Lucy slowly started to raise her hand, questioning herself with each inch that it moved upward. By the time her hand reached shoulder level, and she was ready to pull it back down again, Graham spotted her.

"Lucy?" he asked. "Did you have a question?"

Lucy felt everybody's eyes on her. "Uh, w-well . . . ," she stuttered. "Isn't it, you know, *illegal* to sell beer at a school-sponsored event?"

Rachel shook her head. "This isn't high school anymore, Lucy. This is college."

Lucy looked at Rachel, embarrassed. She nodded nervously but managed to continue her thought. "But there will be *minors* at the dance, right? And *drivers*."

She felt Kent's eyes on her and was unsure what he was thinking. All the confidence that had started to build as she addressed Rachel was beginning to drain again.

Graham sat down at his desk and calmly looked at Lucy. "You've got a good point, and it's something we have to consider. But it's not illegal, so long as all the attendees are carded. In fact, it's not even uncommon. This is a practice that's been done in the past at the university, on many occasions. And there are alumni present, a lot of them, who help monitor consumption. As for the driving issues, we've got Students Against Drunk Driving assisting with taxiing students home. They'll be promoting safe driving all night."

Lucy felt herself relax a little—after all, SADD was a very respected organization. If they were giving their support, perhaps it wasn't as crazy an idea as it sounded. But she couldn't deny the feeling in the pit of her stomach. Was it safe?

A quiet guy named Aaron, who was sitting alone, raised his hand. His hair was wild and spiky and his forearm had a small tattoo of a geometric design. "Everybody knows how to get a fake ID," he said. "As soon as word gets out about the dance, all the minors will go to work on getting one. There's even a kid in my dorm who makes them on his computer."

Rachel nodded and laughed. "That's all the better for us. The more alcohol we sell, the more money we'll make for our charities."

Lucy was so frustrated by Rachel's argument that she actually forgot to be self-conscious. "That may be financially smart, but ethically and legally it's wrong. If there is alcohol at the dance, we have the obligation to make sure that minors can't get it."

Kent nodded in agreement. "Fake IDs could be a problem. That's why they didn't sell beer last year. . . ." He rubbed his head, thinking. Then he looked at Graham. "Why don't we spend the rest of the meeting brainstorming on safety precautions we can take. Then we can postpone the vote until tomorrow, giving everyone a day to think about it."

Graham nodded and Lucy breathed a sigh of relief. For some reason, she trusted Kent. So long as they could find a way to make the dance safe for everybody, she could give her support to the idea. After all, if it'd been done before, what could be wrong with doing it again?

Meanwhile, Ruthie was putting her next plan into action. She was talking on the telephone to Lexie Silver, the coolest girl in school. Just as Ruthie suspected, Lexie was worried that Ruthie's party would be a dud.

"Movie parties are lame-o, unless they're in the dark," Lexie said. "Boys won't grab your hand when the lights are on. They're too chicken."

Ruthie sighed in agreement. "We might as well be playing pin the tail on the donkey."

"Or having an egg toss!" Lexie scoffed.

"Or even worse, musical chairs," Ruthie added with disdain.

Suddenly Lexie gasped. A brilliant idea had just occurred to her. An idea that would save her friend's reputation—and simultaneously boost her own.

"Why don't we throw a Valentine's Day party together, at *my* house? We could play spin the bottle!"

Ruthie shouted in agreement. What could be more rad than throwing a party with Lexie Silver?

FOUR

Later that night, after Lucy had suffered through her first *Star Trek* episode with Tanya, she made her way down the hallway to her room. Just before she reached her door, a group of freshman girls walked out of the room across from hers.

"Hey, Lucy," one of the girls, Priscilla, chirped. "Have you finally got a date to the ball or what?"

Lucy rolled her eyes. "Not even close."

The other girls all clucked and cooed out of pity.

"Maybe it's because you're hanging out with that sci-fi geek," Priscilla said, motioning down the hall. "I mean, her glasses are so thick you can't even tell what color her eyes are."

"They're probably *red*!" one of the girls joked. "Like an *alien's*!"

Another girl nodded. "Yeah, and what's with her hair? Can't that girl buy a comb for her frizz?"

The entire group burst out laughing. But before Lucy could work up the courage to defend her friend, the girls had already disappeared out the exit door. Lucy sighed and walked into her dorm room. She shut the door and leaned against it, suddenly wanting to cry.

But why did she suddenly feel so sad when the day had gone so well? Was it because the girls had made fun of Tanya? Was it because she still didn't have a date? Was it because she felt like she didn't belong in a dormitory full of people who were cooler than she was?

But then she realized something. Those girls weren't cool. They were so insecure that they had to make fun of Tanya—the nicest, most unthreatening girl on campus. *They* were the dorks.

Suddenly there was a knock on Lucy's door.

"Just a minute," Lucy called, hoping it was Tanya. Maybe they could make some popcorn and watch an old movie!

But to Lucy's surprise, the visitor in the doorway wasn't Tanya. It was Kent.

"Uh-uh . . . ," Lucy stuttered. "Hi."

Kent smiled apologetically and ran his fingers through his dark hair. "I'm sorry it's so late. It took me forever to figure out where you lived. . . ."

Lucy shrugged. "Please. It's barely midnight." The words had come out with a hint of flirtation.

Nice work, Luce.

But Kent didn't seem to get the flirtatious part. He spun his watch around and looked at it, shocked that it was, indeed, midnight. "Wow. It *is* midnight." He bit his lip as though worried that his visit was a poor display of manners. "I was at the library," he explained. "I didn't realize it was so late or I would have at least waited until morning. I mean, it's not like I'm here on urgent business or anything. I don't have a life-or-death situation to present you with. I just have a simple question."

Lucy stared at him. If she didn't know

better, she would have thought that he was nervous.

Lucy smiled and opened the door all the way for him to come in. "Have a seat on my friend Bethany's luxurious bed," Lucy said with a grand sweep of her hands across the dorm room, which was empty of any sofa or club chair.

"Who's Bethany?" Kent asked.

"The occupant of this room. She's letting me stay here while she studies in Europe."

Kent nodded. "I didn't think you lived on campus."

Lucy was flattered that he'd noticed her absence.

Kent relaxed a bit and pulled his hands from out of his pockets as he sat down. "Listen, Lucy. . . ." He rested his forearms across his knees and leaned over to look at her.

Lucy felt her heart leap. His eyes were so intent on hers. Maybe he was going to ask her to the dance? She sat down on her bed, drew her legs up under her, and gave him all of her attention.

But then a thought crossed her mind. He could easily be here on ASG business.

She dropped her legs to the floor and crossed them, suddenly professional.

Kent noted the change in her body language and sat up straight. "I'll be quick," he promised.

"You don't have to be quick."

"No, I do. It's midnight and I barely know you."

"Then let's hear it."

Did I just say 'let's hear it'? I'm taking control! This is good.

"You have a boyfriend, don't you?"

"A *what*?"

"A boyfriend. A beautiful girl like you *has* to have a boyfriend. Right?"

"Uh . . . well, not exactly. Why?"

"Because somebody wants to ask you to the ball, and I promised him I'd do his homework for him."

Lucy felt her heart sink. She had let herself get excited after all, and now she was paying the price. She was certain the interested guy was Aaron, the quiet student from ASG. She thought she'd seen him looking at her in the last meeting. Lucy pulled her knees back up under her.

"No, I don't have a boyfriend. Or a date."

Kent's eyes widened. "You're kidding, right? Because I had a bet with him that you were taken."

Lucy forced herself to laugh. "You and some guy are taking bets on me? I don't know whether to be honored or offended."

Kent smiled. "I believe that you should be honored."

Lucy tried to be positive. There was nothing wrong with Aaron. He wasn't her type, but he seemed nice enough. Or maybe it was Graham? He was kind of cute. But not half as cute as Kent. "So who is this guy?"

Kent sighed and opened up his bag. He pulled out his notebook and flipped open a page. On that page was a two-letter word:

Me

Lucy was dumbfounded. For ten whole seconds, she said nothing.

"Well?" Kent said finally. "Since you don't have the boyfriend excuse, you better say yes or make up a dying-aunt story real quick."

Lucy laughed and jumped up off the bed. "I'd be *delighted* to be your date!"

Kent jumped up beside her, his eyes sparkling, as though *he* was the lucky one. "I can't believe it." Then he rubbed his hands together, uncertain of what to say next.

"Oh," he said, remembering something. "We'll be double-dating with Graham."

Lucy immediately thought of Tanya and jumped at the opportunity. "Great! Does he have a date?"

Kent nodded. "He's had the same girlfriend for three years. Her name is Maya. They're practically married. We've rented a limo."

"A limo?" Lucy exclaimed. "I've never been in a limo!"

Kent was pleased by Lucy's reaction and started to say something. But before he could get the words out, his eyes settled on hers and he lost his train of thought. The two sat there, looking at one another, both of them tongue-tied. Finally, Kent smiled and stood up to go. "Well. It *is* after midnight."

Lucy sighed and walked Kent to the door, wishing that time did not exist. "It is," she said softly, and felt goose bumps rise on her skin when his hand brushed hers.

He caught her fingers in his and squeezed them quickly. "Good night, Lucy."

Lucy smiled as he let go of her hand. "Good night."

She watched him walk down the hall, following his broad shoulders and confident walk with her eyes. When he disappeared from view, she shut her door and collapsed on the bed. She couldn't believe her good luck.

Now, how could she tell Tanya?

Back at the Camdens', Ruthie was marching through the house in search of her mother. Once again, she found the twins in their chairs at the table. And once again, the three-year-olds told her nothing about her mother's whereabouts.

Ruthie walked into the backyard and found her mother planting rosebushes along the fence. "Just so you know, nobody's watching the boys."

Mrs. Camden pointed to the intercom walkie-talkie. She could hear the sounds of the two kids munching on their fruit snacks. "I also have the back door open. I can see through the screen just fine, sweetheart."

"Oh." Ruthie stood beside her mother, unsure of how to proceed with the next stage of her plan. It seemed that no matter which direction she moved, her mother was always a step ahead.

"Yes?" Mrs. Camden asked.

"Oh, nothing," Ruthie said, shrugging with exaggerated nonchalance.

Mrs. Camden stood up and studied Ruthie's eyes, which were windows into a mind that was never idle. "So you came out to watch me garden?"

"You got it."

"Because we all know that gardening is a more exciting spectator sport than even NASCAR racing."

"Gardening isn't a sport," Ruthie announced.

Mrs. Camden tapped Ruthie on the nose with her forefinger. "And that, my dear, is the point. What's going on in that busy little head of yours?"

Ruthie shrugged. "I wasn't planning on telling you, but since you insist on dragging it out of me: I'm canceling my Valentine's Day party."

Mrs. Camden looked up, her suspicions confirmed. But for now, she played innocent. "And why wouldn't you tell me this?"

"I didn't want to hurt your feelings."

"And why would my feelings be hurt?"

"Because your standards of cool are so far below my own that I can't in good conscience throw a cheesy party here."

Mrs. Camden shook her head, trying to hide a smile. "Well, I'm sorry to hear that. I was hoping you'd have a party that was ultracool."

"Mom. The word *cool* is so out."

Mrs. Camden's brow creased. "But you just said it."

Ruthie nodded. "Yeah, but I'm a kid. When adults say 'cool,' it screams salt-and-pepper-haired poser."

Mrs. Camden nodded, uninterested in yet another round of adolescent cool school. "And what's the rest of the news that you didn't intend to tell me but can't keep yourself from spilling?"

"If you simply must know," Ruthie said, "Lexie feels so bad about my party that she's throwing one for me."

This was the zinger Mrs. Camden had been waiting for. She began to chuckle.

"What?" Ruthie asked.

And then the chuckle turned into an annoying clicking of Mrs. Camden's tongue, which was accompanied by a rhythmic shaking of both her head and forefinger. "I went to high school with Lexie's mother, and you are absolutely not going to a girl-boy party supervised by Ms. Silver. End of discussion."

Ruthie had known this moment was coming, and had saved all of her inexhaustible energy and newfound vocal shrillness for this exact situation. Ms. Silver was known throughout Glenoak for being a bit wild.

Ruthie opened her mouth and screeched at the top of her lungs, *That's not fair!*"

But after raising four teenagers, Mrs. Camden was a master of preteen cunning. She didn't even flinch. "Then have your party here." She shrugged.

"How can I invite Justin Taylor to my party if it's going to be so lame? You're such a square!"

Ruthie picked up the intercom receiver and threw it across the yard. Unfortunately for her, it hit the picnic table and cracked open with a loud *pop!*

Ruthie froze. The *pop* was not part of the plan. Mrs. Camden was staring a hole through her like no other hole she had stared before.

"I'm sorry," Ruthie said.

"And what else?" Mrs. Camden demanded.

"I'll go pick up the intercom."

"And . . . ?"

"And if it's really broken, I'll buy you a new one."

"Almost there."

"And I'll stop complaining about my party."

"Good."

What neither of them saw was Simon, who was standing at the screen door, laughing.

A few minutes later, after Ruthie had

gone upstairs, Simon walked into the backyard and pulled up two lawn chairs. He motioned for his mom to sit down next to him. Then he handed her a glass of iced tea.

Confused, Mrs. Camden sat down next to her fifteen-year-old son. She smiled. Simon had always acted far older than his years.

"What can I do for you, Simon?"

He leaned over and patted her knee. "Listen, Mom. I know that you and Dad are the parents, and whatever you say goes."

Mrs. Camden nodded. Unlike with Ruthie, she took Simon somewhat seriously. "Let's hear it."

"I think you should take into consideration that it's very hard being a Camden kid—and Ruthie's entering a new stage where it's vitally important that she appears cool when interacting with kids of the opposite gender."

Mrs. Camden nodded. "You think I'm being too harsh?"

Simon threw up his hands. "What's wrong with letting them watch a movie in the dark?"

FIVE

The next day, when Lucy told Tanya about her date with Kent, Tanya surprised her with her excitement. She didn't seem even the least bit jealous. In fact, Tanya asked Lucy if she could help pick out her dress for the ball.

That afternoon, after classes were over, the two girls headed off to the mall. Lucy started to go to one of the cheaper department stores, but Tanya shook her head.

"Oh no, girl. You're going in style."

Lucy looked at Tanya, whose red hair was wild and curly from the humid winter day. "I don't think I've got the cash to hit the other end of the mall," Lucy warned.

Tanya asked how much money Lucy could spend.

"A hundred and fifty dollars," Lucy said.

Tanya nodded. "We'll find you a dress."

"At the nice store?" Lucy asked doubtfully.

Tanya nodded and pulled Lucy through the mall. When the two girls reached the entrance to the expensive department store, Tanya walked straight up to the women's retail counter and asked where they could find the formal wear. The woman behind the counter pointed upstairs and Tanya motioned Lucy onward.

Within seconds, the escalator dropped the girls at the entrance to the nicest formal department Lucy had ever seen. Dresses of every color, material, and style filled row after row of shiny gold racks.

"Wow," Lucy said. "I feel like Cinderella—too poor to afford any of this!"

Tanya laughed and said that together the two would definitely find a bargain. "Hey," Tanya said. "What color do you want?"

Lucy shrugged. "I'm not that picky."

Tanya cut to the chase. "But what color do you *really* want?"

Lucy smiled sheepishly. "Red."

Tanya raised an eyebrow. "Daring. And what fabric?"

Lucy shrugged again, but Tanya wouldn't stand for it.

"What fabric, Lucy?"

"Silk?"

Suddenly Tanya pulled out a long red silk gown with thin spaghetti straps and a full skirt. "Like this?"

Lucy gasped. It was so beautiful. It looked just like the dress from the poster for the Winter Ball. It was the exact dress she'd dreamed of.

"How much?" Lucy's tone was full of dread.

Tanya looked at the price tag. Then she looked at Lucy and shrugged. "Who cares?"

Lucy reached over and grabbed the tag. *"Three hundred dollars?"*

Tanya snatched the dress away and started walking toward the fitting room. "Like I said, who cares?"

Lucy followed her, whining. "I do. There's no point in trying it on."

Tanya opened a dressing room and put the dress inside. "The point is that you want to. So do it."

Lucy sighed and stepped into the dressing room.

Two minutes later, she stepped out, and Tanya shrieked because the gown was so gorgeous. It made Lucy look taller and thinner, and the tapered waist helped accentuate her best features. And there was something about the color: it intensified her blue eyes and contrasted so strongly with her porcelain skin that the effect was striking. The two girls stood in front of the mirror in awe over how perfect the dress was. Lucy really *did* look like a princess in it.

But the magical moment only frustrated Lucy, who threw up her hands in surrender. "Well," she announced, heading back into the dressing room. "Dream over."

Tanya leaned into the doorway. "I'm buying it for you."

Lucy looked at Tanya. "Excuse me?"

"I'd like to," Tanya said. "I've never had a friend like you. I mean, you're so hip—"

Lucy laughed out loud. "Me? I'm the biggest geek on the planet."

Tanya's brow furrowed. "Please. Everywhere you go, the guys notice. But let me finish. You're so hip *and* you're nice. Those two things don't come together very often. And they certainly don't walk into *my* life every day. So I'd like to buy this dress for you. This is your big night. It should be special."

Lucy was dumbfounded. "It's *three hundred dollars*, Tanya. That's book money for the rest of the semester."

Tanya shrugged. "I'm on a full scholarship, Lucy. I even have a living stipend. The college *pays* me to attend. But what do I have to spend the money on? I don't go out, I study. And my parents own a grocery store, so even my food is free."

"Okay," Lucy relented. "We'll each pay for half, but I don't know how to thank you. . . ."

"Just say thank you, and then don't complain about *Star Trek* anymore."

Lucy laughed and nodded. "Okay!

Thank you!" Then Lucy thought of something, and she looked Tanya in the eye. "You know what? *You* are such a cool chick. And I hope that you believe that, because it's true. You're independent, you're brilliant, and you don't really care what other people think. That's so rare, Tanya."

Tanya rolled her eyes. "Unfortunately, I *do* care what people think. I have no style. My hair's a mess. Panache just doesn't come to me like it comes to you."

"Panache?" Lucy laughed. "You've got the best words."

"Elan, dash, flair, verve . . . I don't have it, no matter what you call it."

All at once, Lucy had a great idea. "Let's give you a makeover!" she squealed. "First we'll go to the makeup department, then we'll go to a salon, and then I'll take you on a shopping spree!"

Tanya bit her lip. "You think it'll help?"

Lucy leaned over and pulled off Tanya's glasses. "You have a gorgeous face; you just need some contacts. And this mane of hair could be beautiful. If you could tame it with the right cut, forget about it—the boys will come crawling."

A few minutes later, after the girls had purchased the dress, Lucy dragged Tanya to the makeup counter. She grabbed a stool and sat Tanya down on it. Then she motioned to the consultant behind the counter, who was the most striking young woman Lucy had ever seen.

The consultant walked over to the counter, and Lucy was relieved to see that her expression was kind rather than snooty. "May I help you?" she asked.

Lucy nodded and began her story, which she had slightly altered from the truth in order to make Tanya feel more comfortable. "My friend and I both desperately need dates to the university's Winter Ball. Could you give us a makeover and then point us to the nearest salon? We want to look *fabulous*!"

The young woman laughed. "I'd love to. But I'm a little confused. Aren't you Lucy Camden?"

Lucy raised a surprised eyebrow. "Yes. . . ."

The young woman reached out to shake her hand. "I'm Maya, Graham's girlfriend. I thought we were double-dating?"

Lucy saw Tanya shrink in her chair, feeling more like a nonentity than ever.

How awful for Tanya. The girlfriend of the guy she likes is going to give her a makeover. Ugh.

Lucy nodded at Maya, embarrassed. "Yeah, I am, I just . . ."

Suddenly Maya noticed the red splotches across Tanya's face and put together the puzzle pieces: Lucy was helping Tanya save face. Maya smiled at Tanya, then reached out and squeezed her arm.

"I didn't even go to my freshman ball," Maya said confidingly. "Nobody asked me. I had a horrible case of late-breaking acne. But you . . ." She leaned over and inspected Tanya's face. "You have *exquisite* skin. Model-quality skin. Freckles like yours are in right now. And your pores . . . they're imperceptible. Just wait until I finish with you."

In the Camden kitchen, Mrs. Camden had discussed the movie-party dilemma with Reverend Camden. The two had come up with an acceptable compromise. Mrs. Camden kissed her husband, then walked up the stairs to Ruthie's bedroom. She knocked on the door and Ruthie yelled for her to come in.

"I've got a compromise for you," Mrs. Camden said.

"Wait," Ruthie said, holding up her hand. "I've got an apology for you first. I'm sorry I've been so demanding."

Mrs. Camden looked at Ruthie carefully. "What do you want? Because the compromise I'm about to offer is all you get."

"I don't want anything," Ruthie said. "I just wanted you to know I was sorry."

Mrs. Camden smiled, touched by the gesture. "Thank you, Ruthie, that's very sweet." She leaned over and kissed her daughter's head. "Now here's the compromise: you can turn off the lights in the living room so long as the following lights are on—the hall light . . ."

Ruthie nodded. That was acceptable.

"The light from your father's laptop screen, which we'll move in from his study . . ."

"Yep."

"And I'm going to the store to buy some wall-socket lights. I'll put three of them in the room. And that's it."

Ruthie grinned. "Cool."

Mrs. Camden sat down on Ruthie's bed and put her arm around her daughter. "So you're really happy with that?"

"Absolutely."

"No other requests?"

"Nope."

Mrs. Camden stood up, surprised that it had been so easy. "I want you and your friends to have a great time, Ruthie. You deserve it. You've done so well in school and you're turning into a lovely young lady. I hope it's a great party." She walked to the door and opened it. "Good night, Ruthie."

"Good night, Mom." Ruthie smiled the most angelic smile she could muster.

Just as Mrs. Camden began to close the door, Ruthie feigned a moment of surprise. "Oh, I just remembered. . . ."

Mrs. Camden's smile melted. Had she just let Ruthie fool her again? "Yes?"

"If you could stay upstairs, I'd really appreciate it."

Mrs. Camden pushed the door wider.

"While you're downstairs partying in the dark with your friends?"

Ruthie smiled sweetly. "Then how about the kitchen?"

Mrs. Camden was too tired to negotiate any further. She'd consult with Simon and Reverend Camden in the morning. She shut the door without answering, and Ruthie slid beneath her covers, certain she'd outsmarted her mother again.

Just then, Ruthie heard a ruckus downstairs and climbed out of bed. Somebody was shouting. Was it Lucy? She ran down the stairs, curious to learn what all the hullabaloo was about.

Standing in the foyer was Lucy, who had a long dress bag in hand, which held her new gown. Lucy was shouting for everyone to come look at the dress. She started to unzip the bag as the reverend, Robbie, Mrs. Camden, and Simon all appeared from various rooms in the house.

Suddenly Lucy thought better of it. Why pull the dress out when she could model it for them?

"Wait!" she shouted. "Let me run up and put it on!"

As quickly as Lucy had arrived, she disappeared up the stairs, rushing past Ruthie without even a pat on the girl's head. The family waited in anticipation.

Minutes later, Lucy came down the stairs like a princess descending the winding staircase of a castle. Her gown was long, red, and full, and her golden hair hung long and shiny across the top of it. But more striking were her eyes, which shone with an excitement that the Camdens hadn't seen in a long time.

"Wow," the reverend said.

Robbie nodded and turned to the reverend. "You better keep an eye on her," he joked.

Lucy turned around for them to see the dress from all angles. Then she excitedly explained that her friend Tanya had helped buy the dress for her as a gift, and that her date, the *president of the student body*, was renting a limo for the ball. Not only that, they were double-dating with the coolest couple on campus! It would be the most romantic night of her life!

SIX

The next morning, Lucy dropped by Tanya's room before the charity committee meeting. When Tanya opened the door, Lucy was delighted to find that Tanya had used Maya's makeover tips. Not only was she wearing a daring coral lipstick—which only she, a redheaded autumn, could pull off—she had gone to the optometrist. She had purchased contacts, *and* she had also bought the hip new style of glasses that Maya had suggested. They gave her a dollop of artistic flair. Very cool indeed.

In addition to buying new makeup and glasses, Tanya and Lucy had spent the rest of the afternoon clothes-shopping and salon-hopping. The hairstylist had dramatically layered Tanya's thick mane of curls, so now her hair was not only manageable but ravishing. The stylist had suggested a gel product that turned Tanya's frizzy kinks into long, controlled ringlets.

To top it off, Tanya was wearing low-rise, flat-front orange sport pants. They were wild and rambunctious, with zipper pockets sprawling about in every direction. They screamed, *Look at me, if you dare!* On top, she was wearing a sporty white tank top with thin orange piping across the thick, wide seams. When she stretched, her tight little tummy peeked out just enough to announce its arrival. Finishing off the look was a pair of orange-and-white sneakers with a two-inch sole. Around the sole, little white plastic nubbies spiked out toward the ground.

A miracle had occurred. Tanya Berringer had edge!

"Watch out, ASG!" Lucy said with relish.

Tanya tossed her hair over her shoulder and cocked out her hip in a fabulous display of attitude. "I think you mean, *Watch out, world!*"

The two girls laughed as they made their way across campus, savoring the looks they were getting from other students. Looks that said, *Hey, where have those two starlets been hiding?*

As they approached the student government building, Tanya linked arms with Lucy and pulled her closer. "I don't know why I get so nervous around groups of people. But today I'm going to speak up, speak my mind. I'm going to meet people's eyes and tell them what I think." Tanya gave Lucy a hug. "Thanks for being such a great friend. I feel like I'm a completely new person because of you."

Lucy laughed and waved Tanya's compliment away. "All you needed was a little push."

"You know, I don't ever want to become one of those shallow people who are obsessed with their looks. So you have to promise me you won't let that happen."

"Please," Lucy said. "There's good attitude and bad attitude. You've got good attitude. But the minute you stop talking to people because you're too cool, or judging others because they're not cool enough, then I'll knock you around. Okay?"

The two girls laughed, and Lucy let go of Tanya's arm. "Now go in there and work your makeover magic!"

When the two girls walked into the room, they waited for the moment when everyone would look up and say, *Oh my God, is that Tanya?*

Unfortunately, everyone was too busy scribbling in their notepads to notice.

Lucy looked at Tanya, whose confidence faded visibly. Lucy shook her head and smiled. *Give them time,* her look said. So the two girls grabbed their seats and waited for the others to look up.

Kent was the first one who did. His eyes went straight to Lucy. He smiled.

Then Graham looked up. He nodded at the two girls, but his face was serious and professional. Clearly, he had other things on his mind besides Tanya and her new look.

"I now call the meeting to order," he said.

Which is when everybody else looked up. But instead of noticing Tanya, their eyes remained on Graham.

Lucy looked at Tanya, whose confidence had drained all too quickly. Tanya slunk deeper in her seat, wishing she could disappear completely.

Lucy leaned over and whispered, "Today's the big vote. People are focused on that. It's not about you."

And, in fact, *Lucy* was thinking about the vote. Even though she'd been caught up in clothes-shopping and makeovers, the vote hadn't once left the back of her mind. Today was the most important meeting before the ball. She was waiting to hear everyone's ideas before she would decide whether to vote in favor of selling alcohol or against it.

She squeezed Tanya's arm for support as Graham and Kent stood up to present their idea for dealing with fake IDs. Kent began.

"Graham and I have come up with an elaborate plan for monitoring who will and who won't be sold alcohol. The time we'll have to spend implementing the plan is worth it, because it's basically foolproof."

Graham nodded. "Here's the idea: This committee will sell plastic wristbands, which some of the clubs in Los Angeles use, to people who are twenty-one and over. These wristbands can't be traded between students because once on, they can only be cut off. To get a wristband, each person will have to show us their photo ID at the front door, where a committee member will buckle it onto their wrist. So you see—"

Before Graham could finish his thought, Aaron, the quiet guy with the crazy hair, raised his hand. He was laughing. "So basically, they'll just use their fake IDs to get wristbands!"

Kent shook his head, as he'd already thought of this potential problem. "They can't use fake IDs and here's why: We'll have a computer system set up at the front door to the dance. The system will be connected into the school's main network. When we're presented with a student's ID, we'll type their ID number into the computer—which will prompt their birthdate to appear. If the birthdate in the system matches the one on their card, then the ID is clearly authentic."

Lucy nodded. "So the only way this could fail is if students gained access to the school's main network, then went in and changed their own records."

Aaron shrugged. "And who would go to that much trouble? It's much easier to pay someone to go to the local convenience store and buy you a six-pack."

The group laughed, and Lucy had to admit that the plan sounded extremely solid and safe.

"And we can gain access to the school's network?" Rachel asked.

Kent nodded. "Our ASG sponsor has already cleared it with the vice president."

Lucy looked around the room. Everybody was impressed. Not only would they be able to raise more money for their charities, they would be able to do it in a safe and responsible way.

She leaned over and asked Tanya what she thought, but Tanya hadn't been listening. She was still bummed about the group's reaction—or lack thereof—to her new look.

Lucy snapped her fingers in front of Tanya's face. "Wake up, girl. We've got serious business to attend to. We'll have a pity party later, okay?"

Tanya looked at Lucy and couldn't help but smile. It *was* pretty funny that she let herself get so carried away with her appearance. It was downright silly. What would her Trekkie friends say about such shallowness? It was time for a new attitude!

Tanya sat up and, to everyone's surprise, asked the group if anyone else had any other ideas. Suddenly everyone was looking at her. For the first time. And from the looks on their faces, they all liked what they saw. *Where did this hipster come from?*

After everyone else had pitched their ideas, Tanya spoke up again. "So basically, none of our ideas are better than Kent and Graham's?"

The group laughed and nodded.

"Then I guess it's time for a vote," she said.

Lucy nodded. "I second that motion!"

For the first time since the committee had been meeting, it felt like they were a real, cohesive group. Everyone had found their voice, and nobody was afraid to speak out.

"All in favor?" Graham said.

Lucy waited to see what everyone else did. Other than hers, a unanimous round of hands went up. There wasn't a single look of concern or hesitation on anybody's face. Lucy raised her hand.

"All opposed?" Graham said. Not a single hand was raised. It was final. There would be alcohol at the dance.

Just then, Rachel leaned over to Lucy and whispered, "I heard Kent's taking you to the dance."

Lucy looked at Rachel and grinned. "He is!"

Rachel raised an eyebrow. "Well, aren't you the lucky one."

Lucy's grin softened. *What did Rachel mean by that?*

"Just be careful," Rachel said.

"Why?"

Rachel shrugged. "He's always got a motive."

Confused, Lucy leaned in closer. "I don't know what you mean."

Rachel put her hand over her mouth and leaned in to Lucy's ear. "Let's just say he won't be satisfied with a kiss."

Once again, the elation Lucy had

been feeling turned sour. Sick to her stomach, she gathered her things to go. As she and Tanya headed for the door, Kent stopped her. He leaned over and took her hand in his.

"Do you want to go for a walk tonight?" he asked.

But instead of giving him the warm response she would have given him just ten minutes before, Lucy looked at Rachel, whose eyebrow was arched as if to say, *I told you so*.

Lucy shook her head. "Tanya and I have plans," she said with a quick shrug. "See you tomorrow." Then she grabbed a confused Tanya and hurried her out the door.

Ruthie lay in bed with the phone plastered to her ear. She and Lexie were discussing which movie they should watch at the party. They were in complete agreement on the most important aspect of the plan: the movie needed to be *adult*—otherwise, Justin might think that Ruthie was just a little kid.

Ruthie considered closing her door,

but had just heard her parents fumbling around with the twins downstairs. She was definitely out of earshot.

"How do I rent a sexy movie without my mom and dad knowing about it?" Ruthie asked.

"Do some research," Lexie said. "Find an R-rated movie that has a harmless title and cover."

Ruthie shook her head. "They'll definitely check the rating. We'll get busted for sure. And how would I get it out of the video store anyway? I don't have ID!"

Lexie agreed. This was definitely problematic.

"What about a PG-thirteen movie?" Ruthie asked. "Maybe I could convince the video clerk that I'm thirteen."

Lexie's voice registered her disagreement. "Your lame parents wouldn't even let you watch a PG-thirteen movie."

Ruthie sighed. "Probably not."

"And even if they would, a PG-thirteen movie isn't cool enough anyway. We need an R-rated movie. I mean, you do want to be as popular as me, right?"

Ruthie agreed. "Uh, yeah."

Suddenly Lexie had an idea. "I've got

it! You can rent a little kiddie movie. Then I'll bring over one of my mom's titles. We'll switch the tapes when nobody's looking!"

Ruthie raised both hands and let out a whoop. Her latest obstacle had been swiftly removed from the road to victory, thanks to the wily mind of Lexie. But what new dangers lay ahead?

SEVEN

Later that evening, after Lucy had spent the afternoon pacing back and forth across her dorm-room floor, she decided to talk to her mother about Rachel's comment. She arrived at the Camden home just minutes after supper. Mrs. Camden was in the kitchen with Simon washing dishes.

"Can I talk to you?" Lucy asked, leaning against the kitchen sink.

Mrs. Camden scrubbed at a casserole dish. "Sure," she said, not looking up from the crusty glassware.

Lucy looked at Simon, who was drying dishes slowly and looking out the window, daydreaming about some tenth-grade vision of grandeur. Lucy didn't really want to make the conversation public.

"It's kind of private," she said.

Mrs. Camden and Simon both looked up.

"It is?" they asked in unison.

Lucy rolled her eyes at Simon. "Yes, it is."

Simon grinned. "Great, I'm all ears."

Mrs. Camden's face registered concern. Her middle daughter rarely needed her help unless it was really important. "Let me finish up the dishes, and we'll go upstairs."

Lucy smiled. "Thanks. I'll meet you up there."

As Lucy started up the stairs, Simon shouted after her, "You sure you don't need a second opinion?"

Just then, the reverend came through the kitchen, scurrying little Sam and David out into the backyard. "A second opinion on what?" he asked.

"Nothing," Mrs. Camden said as Simon piped in behind her.

"Lucy's got a secret problem that she'll only discuss with Mom."

"What is it?" his father asked.

"I don't know," Mrs. Camden replied, drying off her hands. "But it's private for now." Then she looked at her husband. "Oh, and by the way . . ."

The reverend's face dropped. "I'm afraid of 'by the ways.' 'By the ways' usually mean you've got work for me to do."

Mrs. Camden smiled. "Just in case everyone's forgotten, the twins' birthdays are on Saturday. Which is the night of Ruthie's Valentine's Day party. I'd appreciate it if you and Robbie could take them out for pizza."

Robbie popped his head in. "Did somebody say 'pizza'? I'm in."

Mrs. Camden smiled at the young man as she passed him on her way up the stairs. "Thanks."

When Mrs. Camden entered Lucy's bedroom, Lucy was sitting on the bed, gnawing at a cuticle, agitated. Mrs. Camden sat down next to her and patted her knee.

"All right, let's talk," she said.

Lucy sighed. "It's probably nothing. It's probably stupid, but . . ."

"Nothing's stupid if it's got you worried."

Lucy nodded. "Remember me telling you about Rachel, the girl on the charity committee?"

Mrs. Camden nodded. "The one who didn't like you?"

"Yeah," Lucy said. "But things have changed since then. She apologized the next day, and she's been really nice since then."

"So what's the problem?" Mrs. Camden asked.

"This morning she said something really weird, and I'm worried it might be true."

Mrs. Camden nodded for Lucy to continue.

"You know how much I like Kent, right?"

"Yes."

"Well, Rachel leaned over at the meeting today and said that I should be careful because he's always got a motive. When I asked her what that meant, she said that he won't be satisfied with just a kiss on the night of the ball."

Lucy looked at her mother, who was waiting to hear if there was more.

"Anything else?" she asked.

Lucy shrugged. "Well, after the meeting, he came and asked me if I wanted to go for a walk with him—you know, at night."

Mrs. Camden nodded. "First of all, it seems perfectly normal to me that he asked you to go for a walk. Your father and I used to love to go walking when we were courting. So I don't think that means anything at all. And second, Rachel may be right about Kent, but it may very well be that *Rachel* is the one with the motive. Maybe she likes him, Lucy, and she wants to scare you away. Or maybe she ran for president last year and lost, so she's trying to tarnish his reputation. Maybe they're having a power struggle over issues with ASG. Regardless of what the truth is, you shouldn't jump to conclusions before you know the whole story."

Lucy nodded. She knew her mother would put everything into perspective. Maybe Rachel *was* the one with the motive. After all, she wasn't friendly with Lucy when they first met. Her behavior wasn't particularly consistent, maybe not even trustworthy. But then again, the first words out of Kent's mouth to Lucy had been about her *underwear*. The *nice stripes* comment wasn't exactly gentlemanly.

Mrs. Camden interrupted Lucy's thoughts. "Even if Rachel's telling the truth, *you* know how to set your own boundaries. It's not as though a guy has all the control on a date. A woman begins sending signals from the very first moment she opens the front door. Make it clear up front what kind of girl you are—don't make any bad decisions—and you'll be fine, Lucy."

Lucy nodded again and wondered if inviting him to sit on her roommate's bed had been the wrong signal. But then again, there weren't many other places to sit. . . .

"Yeah, you're right. I guess I'm upset because I like him so much. It's not that I'm afraid. I just want to believe that he's as perfect as he appears."

"Nobody's perfect, Lucy."

"I know, but with the exception of one thing, he's been such a gentleman and I'll be really disappointed if there's another side to him."

Mrs. Camden put her arms around

Lucy. "I'm glad you came to me, Luce. Sometimes I think you think you're too old and wise to need me anymore."

The two shared a warm hug and then Mrs. Camden pulled away. "I do have one thing to say, though. And I know I don't need to say it, but I'm going to. If anybody offers you a drink, don't take it."

Mrs. Camden waited for Lucy to scoff at the idea. But instead of treating her mother like a paranoid parent who should know better, Lucy sighed.

"I meant to tell you that we're selling alcohol at the dance."

Mrs. Camden's jaw dropped open in shock. "You're *what*?"

"I mean, the *student government* is selling alcohol."

Mrs. Camden sat up and crossed her own arms. "You mean to tell me that the school is providing alcohol to its own students? That's outrageous."

Lucy suddenly felt defensive and stood up. "Mom, it's not outrageous. It's common in college. They card the minors. It's not like a bunch of teenagers will be running around boozing it up on the school dime."

"Then what will it be like? I was just watching a news program on teen drinking. Do you know how easy it is to get a fake ID?"

"Mother, we've got it all figured out. We're cross-referencing student IDs with their birth records in the school computer system. They *can't* use fake IDs."

"We?" Mrs. Camden said. "You mean *you* had something to do with this?"

"I'm on the committee, Mom. We voted and the vote was unanimous. We're selling it to raise money for charities. It's a proven fact that selling alcohol will raise three to four times more money than not selling it. It's for a good cause. And the system we have in place is safe. I wouldn't have voted for it if I hadn't really thought it over. You've taught me better than that."

Mrs. Camden sighed and stood up. "Well, I did raise you, and if you really feel that this is right, then either I've failed or I'm wrong. I don't know which one."

Lucy took her mother's face in her hands and looked her in the eyes. "You haven't failed. You're the best mom a girl could ask for. But I'm not in high school anymore."

Mrs. Camden nodded and added quietly, "Nor are you an adult, Lucy. You're still eighteen. *Eighteen.* If you drink at the dance—"

Lucy cut her mother off. "I'm not going to drink at the dance! That's not what this is about. It's about me being honest with you. I thought you trusted me?"

"I do trust you," Mrs. Camden said. "I just don't trust twenty-one-year-old student body presidents who want to take eighteen-year-old girls out to drinking parties in limousines."

Lucy couldn't help the scoff that came out of her mouth. "*You're* the one who said not to jump to conclusions!"

Mrs. Camden threw up her hands. "That was before I knew there would be beer provided by the school!"

Just then, Lucy's father poked his head in the room. Behind him, the entire family was gathered in the hallway, curious about what could have so upset the two.

"There's going to be beer at the dance?" he asked.

Matt, Lucy's oldest brother, who had

just dropped in for a visit, entered the room. "Yep," he answered his father, plopping down on the bed. "It's all over town. A school-sponsored keg party!"

Lucy scowled at Matt, who threw up his hands. "What? It's true! And from what I hear, you're on the committee that voted it in."

The reverend surprised everyone in the room by holding up a calming hand and saying, "I don't know all the facts yet, but this is Lucy's issue, not yours. She made a decision, and it's hers to stick by." He looked at Lucy. "If there's fallout from that decision, she'll face the consequences, like the daughter we raised her to be. Now everybody off to bed."

And with that, he scooted Lucy, her siblings, and the visiting Lexie out of the room. Then he turned to Mrs. Camden and closed the door behind them.

As Lucy left the house to get a ride back to school with Matt, Ruthie and Lexie returned to Ruthie's bedroom to finalize their party plans.

"So what movie are you going to rent?" Lexie asked Ruthie.

"Fairy Tale Friends." Ruthie said with a chuckle. "Isn't that the cheesiest movie you've ever heard of?"

Lexie nodded. "It's perfect. Your mom will never guess!"

Ruthie grinned wickedly. It *was* pretty sneaky, getting a movie that was so clearly infantile. Her mother would be relieved to know that it was rated G, and consequently feel less obliged to hang out in the living room.

"How about *your* movie?" Ruthie asked. "Did you go through your mom's collection? Did you find something sexy?"

Just then, Mrs. Camden's door opened down the hall. She stuck her head out, her ears twitching like a rabbit's. "What did you say, Ruthie?"

Ruthie crossed her arms. *"Hello,* the name of the person I'm talking to. *Lexie."*

Mrs. Camden walked into the hallway and looked straight at Ruthie. "I know what you said, and you are too young to be using that word." She returned to her bedroom.

The door shut again, and Ruthie stood up and closed her own door.

"Your mom is *so* beat!" Lexie said.

Ruthie dropped back onto the bed. "Tell me about it."

Lexie sighed. "So anyway, I'm bringing a very cool movie."

Suddenly Ruthie furrowed her brow, thinking. "The only part of the plan that could be problematic is the location of my mom and dad. I've asked my mom to hang out in the kitchen, but she hasn't agreed yet. I'm being extra helpful around the house, so I think everything will work out."

"And your dad?"

"It's Saturday night. He always works on his sermons for the Sunday service. We'll just have to stay alert. When the study door opens, you're in charge of the remote. Turn off the power and I'll act like there's something wrong with the TV."

The two girls high-fived each other as a honk was heard outside. Ruthie looked out the window and saw Lexie's mom in her red convertible.

"Gotta go," Lexie said, grabbing her vinyl neon yellow backpack. "Wanna walk me out? You can check out my mom's new car."

Two minutes later, Ruthie was sitting in the backseat of Ms. Silver's new Audi convertible, and Ms. Silver was explaining how fast it could go.

"Wanna go for a quick spin around the block?" Lexie's mom asked.

Just then, Mrs. Camden's bedroom window opened and Ruthie spotted her mother's fluffy blond head peering down at the threesome. She waved sweetly, but Ruthie could tell she had an agenda other than socializing.

"By the way, Ruthie, there will be no unsuitable movies at the party. Pass it on to whoever needs to hear."

Blast it all! Ruthie felt like she was up to bat in the ninth inning and Mrs. Camden was on the mound. Bases were loaded. Full count. Would Ruthie strike out or hit a home run?

EIGHT

The next night, Lucy considered calling Kent. Maybe she had acted strangely when he asked her to go for a walk. Maybe she *was* being paranoid. After all, Kent had been nothing but friendly toward her. But then again, maybe calling him would be too forward?

Lucy, the nineties are passé. A girl can call a boy without sending the "wrong" signals.

Lucy picked up the phone and dialed the campus directory. But as soon as the operator connected her, her heart started pounding. What would she say? That she was sorry she turned him down? Maybe it would be awkward to apologize for such a thing. Girls have alternate plans all the time. Girls don't have to drop their plans just because guys ask them out. If anything, it probably made her more attractive.

Why do I care? Why am I doing all this guesswork? Why can't I just talk to him?

Before anybody answered, Lucy hung up the phone. She was way overanalyzing this. She needed to just let events unfold. If Kent tried anything with her, she could address it then. If he didn't, she'd be glad she never brought it up. Right?

There was a knock at the door, and Lucy started toward it, her heart pounding again. What if it was him?

She opened the door. Aaron, the guy with the spiky hair, stood outside.

"Hey, Aaron, what's up?" she said.

He started to say something and then stopped himself. It was almost like he had stuttered. Was he nervous in front of her, too? What was happening to all the guys on campus?

"Uh . . . are you busy?"

Lucy shook her head. "Not at all."

"You're sure? I mean, uh, I could

come back at a better time. It's kinda rude to show up out of the blue."

Lucy smiled and opened the door. "Please. We're in a dormitory. Strangers knock more often than friends do!"

"Cool, thanks." Aaron walked in and sat down on Bethany's bed. "Is it okay to sit here?"

Lucy thought about her earlier concerns and shrugged them off. "Sure. There isn't much furniture, so it's a bed or a desk chair."

Aaron smiled, and he seemed to relax a bit, although Lucy noticed that he kept twisting the leather bracelet that was on his wrist. It seemed like a nervous habit. Kind of like Kent twisting his watch.

"So what's up?" Lucy asked, smiling. "Is it about the ball?"

Aaron nodded. "Uh, yeah, actually . . . it is."

Suddenly Lucy realized that his face had turned red.

Oh no, he wants to ask me out.

"You're sure now is a good time?" he asked again.

And then Lucy realized why he kept

assuming it was a bad time to talk: she was completely distracted. She was thinking about Kent and the phone call. How rude of her. She looked at him, giving him her full attention.

"So is this about the committee, or about . . . a date?"

Aaron twisted the bracelet, surprised she had been so forward. "A date."

Lucy smiled gently. "I'm so flattered, Aaron, really. If you'd asked me four days ago, I would have—"

Aaron looked confused. "Asked you what?"

"Aren't you asking me out?"

His red cheeks became redder. "No. I was wondering if you knew anything about Tanya's plans."

Now it was Lucy's turn to be embarrassed. She laughed out loud. "Am I egocentric or what?" She shook her head and looked at him again. "So you want to ask Tanya to the ball?"

Aaron nodded. "Do you think she's got a date?"

Lucy was ecstatic. "I know she doesn't. You should definitely ask her!"

He sighed and unhooked the bracelet,

then put it in his pocket. "You think she'd go out with someone like me?"

"Why wouldn't she?"

He shrugged. "I'm a little different, if you know what I mean."

Lucy laughed. "So is she. She's a sci-fi geek and she listens to old heavy-metal music."

Aaron's eyes lit up. "Really?"

Lucy nodded solemnly. "But don't tell her I told you."

"That's so gnarly!" He stood up, putting the bracelet back on. "Do you know where she lives?"

Lucy walked to the door and opened it. She leaned out and pointed down the hallway to Tanya's door. "See that picture of the Borg Queen?"

Aaron nodded vigorously. "She's so wicked."

Lucy looked at him. "Tanya or the Borg Queen?"

"Uh, both. Isn't it obvious?" He said this as though it were a good thing.

Lucy pushed him down the hallway. "Go get her, tiger."

Three minutes later, Lucy heard the theme song to *Star Trek: The Next*

Generation reverberating through the hallway. Tanya had met her match.

Meanwhile, the Camdens' phone was ringing off the hook. Every fifth grader in Glenoak was calling the house about Ruthie's Valentine's Day party, and Mrs. Camden was concerned that Ruthie had invited more than her twelve-person limit.

Ruthie crossed her heart and verbally hoped to die. "I swear I only invited twelve people, but sometimes word gets around and other people just decide they want to come."

Mrs. Camden slid her pot roast and potatoes in the oven. "Well, you better help them undecide, because the living room can't hold more people than that."

Ruthie's next sigh was more melodramatic than the previous one. "Do you know how hard it is to tell nerds who never get invited to parties that they can't come to yours? It's downright cruel, don't you think?"

Mrs. Camden smiled at Ruthie. "I'll tell you what. For every person you have to turn away, I'll write up a personal invitation to Sunday's church service. Then they won't feel left out."

Ruthie gagged and Mrs. Camden turned to her.

"Listen, Ruthie. You agreed to stop complaining about your party and to have a better attitude. We finalized the rules yesterday, and now you're not following them. I know it's hard to tell people they can't come, but you have to. We can't afford food for fifty people, and I don't feel right having one chaperone for so many kids."

Ruthie sat down at the table and pretended to think it over. "All right. I'll call everybody right now and tell them they can't come. I'll even pass out church invitations if you want."

Mrs. Camden looked at her daughter with suspicion. "Really?"

"Sure, if you'll make them."

Mrs. Camden thought it over. "Maybe I will."

Ruthie stood up from the table and started up the stairs. "Great." When she reached the landing, she stopped for dramatic effect, then turned back around.

"Oh, and, Mom . . . ?"

Mrs. Camden turned the oven to 375 degrees, then looked upward as if to say, *Why me, God?* Sometimes it was just too difficult to fight Ruthie. She *never* gave up.

"Have you decided where you'll be staying during the party?"

Mrs. Camden looked at her daughter. "Because I know how important this is to you, Ruthie, I'll stay in the kitchen. But I do have ears."

Ruthie threw a fist up in the air. "Yes!"

The ball was flying toward the center-field fence.

NINE

The day of Ruthie's Valentine's Day party had finally arrived. In just four more hours, the guests would begin to arrive. Ruthie could hardly contain her excitement as she sat in the passenger seat of the family minivan. Her father was driving her and Lexie to the video store to pick out their movie.

Ruthie looked in the backseat at Lexie and winked conspiratorially. This was in the bag.

But the reverend was almost as good as his wife at sensing Ruthie's forays into mischief. He had to admit, though, that he had a harder time disciplining her than he did his other children. Maybe it was because she was younger, so it seemed as though she couldn't really get into serious trouble. Or maybe he was mellowing in his old age.

Or more likely, maybe his daughter had him wrapped around her little finger.

"Let's have a quick talk about your party, Ruthie," he said.

Ruthie rolled her eyes at Lexie, who returned the gesture with an exaggerated heave of her shoulders. This family gave more lectures than all the teachers in all of the Glenoak school district combined.

"I'd love to," Ruthie said.

"I've just noticed that you've been testing your mother all week."

"Oh yeah, that." Ruthie had learned that honesty was the best policy with her dad. He appreciated honesty more than her mother did. Her mother didn't give brownie points for honesty if the truth was only a means to an end. Which it generally was.

"I want you to be on your best behavior tonight. No tricks, okay?"

"I've only got one," she quipped.

Her dad couldn't help but grin. "You

know I'm serious. Make this night an easy one on your mother."

Ruthie nodded and crossed her heart. "I promise."

"And one other thing, Ruthie."

"Name it and it's yours."

"You need to thank your mother for letting you have this party. I don't think you remember what she's given up to let you have this."

Ruthie bit her lip, thinking. Come to think of it, she didn't know what her mother had given up.

"You mean Valentine's Day dinner with you?"

Her father shook his head. "Besides that. Although that's a good guess."

"Is there some dumb mom-movie on Lifetime?"

The reverend shook his head again.

"I guess you need to spoil the suspense and spill the beans. I have no idea."

"It's the twins' birthday."

Ruthie sat up in her seat. How had she forgotten Sam and David's birthday? Every year they had a big birthday party on Valentine's Day—and all of Ruthie's older siblings had to drag their dates over for cake and ice cream. It was her mother's favorite day. Now Ruthie felt bad.

"I forgot," she admitted. "I can't believe Mom let me have this party."

Her father smiled. He knew there was a heart underneath all those machinations. "So you'll remember to thank her when you get home tonight?"

Ruthie nodded. She absolutely would remember.

"Oh, and one last thing," her father said. Ruthie looked up, for some reason concerned that this last thing might be a big thing. As in, an *I'll be watching the movie with you tonight* thing.

"What?" Ruthie asked, terrified.

"Robbie and I are taking the boys out for pizza. So Mom's the only chaperone."

Ruthie couldn't hide the wicked smile that crept across her face. In the back seat, Lexie kneed Ruthie through the seat cushion. Seriously, could this night get any better?

Across town, Lucy was preparing for her big night. The Winter Ball had arrived!

Lucy heard a knock on her door and

opened it to find Tanya in her gorgeous emerald gown. She was wearing her new contacts, and Lucy couldn't believe how beautiful Tanya looked.

"Aaron's going to flip out," Lucy said. "You look unbelievable."

Tanya spun around in her gown, then looked Lucy up and down. She was still in her robe.

"What are you waiting for?"

"It's hard to zip up my dress without help."

"So get in it."

Lucy was excited just thinking about it. She reached for the dress bag and unzipped it. Inside was the astounding red gown. She pulled it out with as much care as she would a baby. She turned to Tanya.

"I can't thank you enough. I really feel like a princess tonight."

Tanya shook her head. "No more thanks. Just enjoy it. Now put it on!"

Lucy squealed as she unzipped the dress and stepped into it. As she pulled it up, she could hear the music of the ball, could see the dancing couples, could hear the sound of Kent's voice. . . .

"Wow," Tanya said as she zipped it up and took a step back to appreciate the final result. "Now that your hair's fixed, you look even more amazing than before. I didn't think that was possible!"

Lucy stepped in front of the mirror and smiled. Then she turned to Tanya. "Are you ready for the crowning jewel?"

Tanya waited for Lucy to pull whatever surprise gem she had from out of her bag. But when Tanya saw what Lucy retrieved, she was breathless. It was a diamond necklace.

"Where did you get that?"

Lucy handed it to Tanya, who helped her put it on. "My mother inherited it from her mother. All my life, I've begged her to let me wear it. And all my life, she would say, *We can talk about that in five or ten years*. But tonight was the first night she agreed to loan it to me. In fact, I didn't even ask her, she offered."

Lucy looked in the mirror again and couldn't believe how brightly it sparkled against her skin.

"Now you *really* look like royalty."

Just then, there was a knock on the

door. Tanya ran to open it and Maya stood outside in a sophisticated white gown. A strand of pearls hung close to her neck, and her hair was pulled back in a tight bun. She looked like a Spanish duchess. In her hand she clutched her makeup bag. It was time for Maya to work her magic on Lucy and Tanya.

The three girls squealed at how amazing they all looked. Then Lucy noticed some girls from her hallway peeking in. They were all in their gowns.

"Where did you get that gorgeous necklace?" Priscilla shouted.

Another girl, the same one who had made fun of Tanya's hair, now exclaimed that Tanya's long ringlets were as romantic as a Lord Byron poem.

"Wait!" a girl in a pink dress shouted, and Lucy realized that she was one of the photographers from down the hall, the one who had her pictures plastered to her doorway. The girl ran into the room with a camera and took a quick shot.

Then she looked at Maya and her makeup bag. "Are you telling me that you guys have your own makeup artist? And I thought *I* was cool." She ran back out as the other girls laughed and headed back to their rooms.

Lucy couldn't help but feel exhilarated by their attention. But she also knew that had she and Tanya not looked so attractive, they would have been ignored. This realization made Lucy cherish Tanya's and Maya's friendship all the more.

Maya set Lucy's desk chair down in front of the mirror and plugged in a makeup light. "Okay, who's first?"

Suddenly Lucy noticed that Tanya had started pacing across the room. But she wasn't pacing like a normal person. She was pacing quickly, as though suddenly filled with anxiety. Lucy laughed at her friend's quirks. "Are you nervous, Tanya?"

But Tanya didn't answer. Instead, she held her hands out in front of her and shook them. Then she closed her eyes and took a deep breath. Lucy exchanged a look with Maya. Maybe Tanya was always like this before big events?

All of a sudden, Lucy noticed that little beads of sweat had started forming on

Tanya's brow. She went to Tanya and took her hand. "Are you okay?"

When Tanya opened her eyes, there were tears in them.

Worried, Lucy nudged her. "Here, sit down." Maya brought a desk chair to her.

"I'm sorry," Tanya whispered. "I'm sorry I'm such a freak."

Lucy squatted next to her, and Maya brought Tanya a cold washcloth.

"Just tell me what it is," Lucy said gently.

Tanya took a breath and looked up. "I can't be around girls like that all night."

Lucy smiled, suddenly realizing how intimidating groups of girls could be. "You'll be fine," Lucy assured her. "We'll be at the dance, just feet away from you, all night."

Tanya sniffled, then admitted that she had other concerns. Big concerns. "I've never had a date before. I don't know what to do."

Lucy touched Tanya's face, wiping away the tear that had started to roll down her cheek. "You're afraid?"

Tanya nodded. "I'm bad enough with big groups of people, especially people I don't know. But a date . . . I'm sick to my stomach right now."

Maya took Tanya's hand and leaned down next to Lucy. "Do you know the story of 'The Ugly Duckling'?" Maya asked.

Tanya nodded.

"Well, that was me. I was the tall, skinny girl with the gawky knees and elbows. And to top it all off, I'm part Mexican."

"What's wrong with being Mexican?" Tanya asked.

"Well, when you go to an all-white prep school, there's a lot wrong with it. The kids teased me for everything. My height, my skin, my name. And I *hated* going to things like dances, so I didn't. I just stayed home."

"And what happened?" Tanya asked.

"I grew into my body, into my mind, and even into my looks—just like you're doing now."

Tanya scoffed. "I haven't grown into my looks. I've just bought things to cover them up."

Lucy shook her head. "That's not true. You've stopped hiding behind your glasses and your hair. It's like you've stepped out from behind a door. You're beautiful, Tanya."

Maya nodded, gently touching Tanya's arm. "It's going to take a while to believe it, because all your life you've been the 'ugly' one. And you're scarred by that, and you can't believe that anybody would actually want to hang out with you. But take it from me, people do. And the sooner you start to believe it, the sooner you'll be able to accept all the wonderful things that are happening to you."

Tanya wiped her wet eyes and stood up. She looked in the mirror. "I just wish I could be as self-assured as you two are."

Now it was Lucy's turn to laugh. "You think *I'm* self-assured? I was scared to knock on your door just a week ago. I didn't think you'd want to eat breakfast with me. And I'm terrified to go out with Kent tonight."

Maya and Tanya looked at Lucy, surprised. Lucy took a deep breath. She had decided not to tell anybody about Rachel's remark, but after everything that Tanya had shared, she felt compelled to do so.

She explained the entire chain of events to the two girls and was surprised when Maya laughed. "Rachel is Kent's ex-girlfriend, Lucy. She's jealous of every attractive girl in ASG. Graham says she even threw a glass of wine at Lindsey, the class treasurer, because she sat down next to Kent at a party!"

Maya grabbed her makeup brush and began dusting Lucy's face with powder. "And she's got good reason to be jealous of you, Lucy. You've got all the depth that she lacks."

Lucy heaved a sigh of relief. "So you don't think he's going to try anything?"

Maya laughed. "Kent is the most well-mannered guy on campus. That's not to say he's perfect, but he's certainly a gentleman."

Lucy was about to ask what wasn't perfect about Kent when Tanya jumped in.

"What about Aaron?" Tanya said. "Is he a gentleman? I don't even know how to kiss."

But before Maya could answer, limousine lights illuminated the window of Lucy's dorm room. The lights of Aaron's car immediately followed. The three girls screamed. They'd spent so much time talking, they hadn't even noticed that an hour had gone by. They weren't even close to being ready.

Five minutes later, Kent, Graham, and Aaron were sitting on Lucy's bed in their tuxedos, waiting for Maya to finish her magic.

And the wait was well worth it.

At Camden party headquarters, Ruthie and Lexie were upstairs. Once again, Ruthie considered closing her door but thought better of it. If Mrs. Camden saw a closed door, she would be sniffing around every two minutes.

Ruthie opened up the movie case of *Fairy Tale Friends* and popped out the tape. She handed the tape to Lexie, who threw it under a pillow and then retrieved a movie case from inside her bag—the case of the popular R-rated movie *Love Like No Other*.

Lexie quickly opened the R-rated case and took out the movie. She handed the tape to Ruthie, who slid it into the case for *Fairy Tale Friends*.

Ruthie lowered a mischievous eyebrow. "If Mom finds out, I can blame it on the video store! I'll tell her they switched the tapes and I didn't notice!"

Lexie nodded and grabbed the G movie from under the pillow. This she deftly placed in the R movie case, which she put in her bag. Then she slid this "evidence" underneath Ruthie's bed.

Ruthie grabbed her football trophies from her dresser, bent down, and shoved them in front of the bag. If anyone decided to look under the bed, they'd have to get through the trophies first.

The two girls ran downstairs and placed the G-rated movie on top of the television set as Reverend Camden and Robbie rushed by with the twins.

"Have a great party, Ruthie!" Robbie called.

Ruthie's dad ran into the living room and kissed his daughter's head. "Remember what I said. No problems."

Ruthie put her arm around Lexie and the two did the Girl Scouts' honor sign in unison. That's exactly what both girls were hoping for: no problems.

TEN

Once outside, the chauffeur opened the door for Lucy and Maya, who lifted up the corners of their skirts and climbed inside. Lucy was surprised to see that the interior didn't have seats that were in rows but that they lined each wall of the limo's back section, forming a rectangle.

Lucy grabbed the seat closest to the door, and Maya took the one across from Lucy. The two girls were facing one another and had plenty of room on each side of them for their dates.

In the center of the limo, rising up from the floor between the two girls, was a bar. Lucy could just see Maya's head over the top of it. They raised their eyes in excitement at one another. How had their dates found a limo like this in Glenoak?

Once both girls were in, Kent and Graham followed. The chauffeur shut the door, and the two guys sat down next to their dates, their eyes glistening with evident pride. Clearly, they had paid a lot of money to make this night a special one.

Lucy pulled at her dress, which had gathered up beneath her legs. She didn't want it to wrinkle. Kent noticed her shuffling about.

"Are you comfortable?" he asked. "What can I do?"

Maya was right. He was a gentleman.

"It's okay, I'm fine," she said.

"Is it your dress?" he asked. "Are you worried that the silk might crinkle?"

Lucy looked at him, amazed that a guy would notice such a small detail. But it made sense when she thought about it. Kent was a detail-oriented guy. This was something that had always attracted her to him. Not only did he run a two-hundred-member organization with incredible efficiency, he also had planned a perfect, romantic evening for the four of them. And he always looked perfectly put together: clean shaven, creased slacks, starched shirt. Yet he was still extremely masculine. He smelled amazing.

"How do you know this dress is silk?" she asked him, teasing. "You're a guy."

"I know a lot of things that would surprise you. Like that day in the rainstorm. You were wearing white linen."

"And red stripes," Lucy groaned.

Kent laughed. "You know, it was really out of line for me to tease you like that."

Lucy nodded, feigning seriousness. "Maya said you were a real gentleman, but that *was* a little coarse of you—being a student body president and all."

Kent nodded and raised his hand. "I did have a good reason, if you'd like to know it."

Lucy's curiosity was piqued. She nodded. "Okay?"

"Well, I've spent all semester trying to get your attention and you've never once looked my way—"

"You have?" Lucy interrupted.

"Yeah! I can't believe you've never noticed. And then suddenly I had my opportunity. You were all alone, walking

through the quad in the rain. It was perfect. I imagined myself pulling up beside
you on my impressive mountain bike,
saying something really romantic, and
then parking my bike and walking you to
the cafeteria. But the closer I got, the
more nervous I became. By the time I
was actually within shouting distance, I
was pedaling as fast as I could. And then
before I knew it, I was almost past you,
and I had to think of something fast. The
first thing that came to mind was the very
last thing I saw . . . the, well, you know—"

"The infamous stripes," Lucy said.

Kent laughed, shaking his head at
himself. "The infamous stripes."

Lucy looked at Kent, whose dark
brown eyes perfectly matched his hair.
Set against the black tuxedo, he looked
like the offspring of some resurrected line
of French nobility. He was so dark and
handsome. She felt a shiver of excitement
run through her. Why had she been nervous before?

Just then, they heard laughter from
the other side of the bar. They looked up
and Graham and Maya were waving.

"Hey, over here! Remember us?" Graham joked.

"What?" Kent asked, clueless.

Maya rolled her eyes. "The two of you are so into your conversation, you've forgotten us. We have to toast the night."

"Now stop whispering and uncork the bottle," Graham said.

Lucy felt her heart stop.

The bottle?

She looked at Kent, who was now opening up the refrigerator. Her heart sank farther when she saw three champagne bottles sitting inside.

Lucy looked to Maya for help, but Maya was pulling wineglasses out of the bar's cabinet. She raised an eyebrow at Lucy and handed her a glass.

"To romance!" Maya said, sounding like there was nothing to be concerned about.

Kent took a glass and clinked Lucy's empty one. "To romance!" He tried to meet her eyes, but Lucy couldn't help looking away. She felt sick to her stomach, just like she had the day Rachel had whispered those awful words.

"Hey!" Graham said. "No toasting until there's gold in the glass."

Kent touched Lucy's arm. "Are you okay?" he asked quietly.

Lucy swallowed and looked back at him. She forced a smile.

I can't ruin a night like this. Not after he's done so much to make it so perfect.

"I'm fine," Lucy lied.

Kent held one of the bottles in his hand. "It's the champagne, isn't it?"

Lucy started to say yes, but Maya jumped in.

"What's wrong with the champagne?"

Kent sighed. "I was worried this would happen, that it would ruin the whole night."

Lucy shook her head. "It's okay, really, just . . ."

"Just what?" he asked tenderly.

She held out her glass. Maybe she would just hold it. "Just pour me a glass."

Kent leaned in closer, making sure that he could see into Lucy's eyes. "Really, it's okay. I can tell you don't want it, so don't drink it."

She could tell he was sincere, and Lucy's fear began to fade. She smiled and nodded. "You're right, I don't."

Now Maya was frustrated. She looked at Lucy, confused. "I don't understand. You're a champagne snob?"

Kent held up the bottle and nodded. "She has every right to be when I bring this in. It's not even three weeks old."

Lucy couldn't believe it: they thought she didn't want the champagne because it wasn't vintage enough. Was she really so out of touch? Maybe everybody drinks in college? Everybody but her.

Maya grabbed the bottle and started to pour. "I think it's a fabulous champagne, and I think Lucy should get over her snobbery and drink it."

Lucy started to hold out her wineglass, but Kent stopped her. He shrugged his shoulders.

"I know it's corny, Lucy, but I just didn't think officers and committee members should be drinking on the night of the ball. It seems irresponsible."

Confused, Lucy looked at the bottle.

And then she laughed out loud.

It was *sparkling apple cider,* not champagne at all!

She looked at Kent again, who was embarrassed.

"I know it's unsophisticated," he continued. "But I also felt wrong about having alcohol around a minor, and not only that—"

Lucy reached up and put her hand over Kent's mouth. Then she held out her glass.

"Pour," she ordered.

"Wh-wh-what?" he stuttered from behind her grip.

Lucy was laughing harder now. "I thought it was real champagne. Now pour."

Now Maya was laughing. "We were just kidding when we called the cider 'champagne.' You thought he wanted you to drink *real* champagne even though you're only eighteen and he's a school officer? That explains the look on your face!"

The worried brow on Kent's face was replaced by an overwhelming smile. He picked up the bottle of sparkling cider and poured as Maya and Graham shoved in with their own glasses.

Thank goodness.

Just then, the limo pulled to a stop and the foursome looked out. They were at the dance, and what they saw amazed them. The decorating committee had done an incredible job. A red carpet lined the sidewalk and spotlights danced about like the lights at a big Hollywood movie premiere.

The chauffeur came around to open their door.

"This is so perfect," she whispered to Kent.

As Lucy and her date climbed out, the largest spotlight of all settled on them, illuminating the gorgeous couple for everyone to see.

What could possibly go wrong on a night like this?

Ruthie's party was rocking and rolling. Ten kids now stood in the kitchen, munching on the chips and salsa that Mrs. Camden had bought. There were only two kids left to arrive—and one of them was Justin.

Lexie leaned against the counter and crossed her arms. *What if he doesn't show?* she mouthed to Ruthie.

Ruthie shot Lexie a *Put a sock in it* look. How socially inept was Lexie to throw that thought out as a possibility? What if the other kids had deciphered her words? Ruthie didn't want them to know that the success of her party rested solely on his arrival.

Just then, the doorbell rang. Ruthie and Lexie raced for the door, both of them struggling to keep their feet in their chunky open-toed shoes, which gave them each an additional two inches of height.

Ruthie reached the door first and flung it open. Outside stood the moderately popular Lily, a girl from their class who was known for raising pet rabbits. This alone made her house a popular stomping ground for neighborhood kids. What was more fun than playing with bunnies? But then again, Ruthie and her friends were almost teenagers—and their fascination with pets was rapidly being replaced by a fascination with each other. Lily's popularity was declining.

Ruthie's face fell, but Lexie's brightened. It was almost as if Lexie didn't want Justin to arrive.

As Lily made her way to the kitchen, Lexie commented that Ruthie's purple shoes didn't match her baby-blue toe-nails. Ruthie scoffed that matching was overrated and boring. Lexie argued the point, saying her own outfit matched perfectly. Ruthie retorted that Lexie's color scheme was an exercise in monotony.

But Ruthie couldn't help worrying that she had picked the wrong toenail polish.

What would Justin think?

"I don't think he's coming," Lexie whispered.

Ruthie spun around. "Are you trying to ruin my party?"

Lexie shook her head in disbelief. "Uh, no! I'm your best friend, duh!"

Before the two could argue further, the doorbell rang and the two girls raced for the door again. Ruthie reached the doorknob first. She looked out the window and grinned. A lanky blond-haired boy stood outside with his hands in his jean pockets. She was surprised to see that his mother was standing beside him.

"It's him!" she said triumphantly.

Lexie ran her fingers through her black mane and tossed it back over her shoulders. "Good."

Ruthie opened the door—and curled her little baby-blue toes in like a turtle hiding its head in its shell. He held a large red-and-pink present in his hand.

"Hi," Ruthie said sweetly as Mrs. Camden came down the stairs.

Justin's mom stepped inside and held her hand out to Mrs. Camden, who shook it. "I'm Jane Taylor. I hope I'm not being a stick-in-the-mud, but is it okay if I pick Justin up at ten?"

Lexie made a nasty face at Ruthie. *Ten o'clock? Justin has to be home that early? What a loser!*

Mrs. Camden shook Jane's hand and smiled.

"The party's over at ten."

Lexie's face soured even more, but Ruthie ignored it. She was focused on the blue-eyed boy with the down-turned face who now stood in front of her. He was wearing a Los Angeles Dodgers cap pulled down low over his eyes. He smiled shyly.

"Happy Valentine's Day, Ruthie." His voice was soft as he held the present out to her. She took it in her arms. But instead of thanking him or opening it, Ruthie was strategizing.

"You didn't need to buy me a gift," she said, one eye on him and the other eye on Lexie. "The only gift I need is you next to me on the couch."

Mrs. Camden's mouth dropped in horror. "Ruthie!" She looked at Mrs. Taylor apologetically. But before she could apologize for Ruthie's forwardness, Lexie grabbed Justin's hand and started pulling him into the room.

"And I'll sit on the other side of you," Lexie exclaimed with a bossy toss of her raven locks.

Ruthie screeched and reached for Justin's free hand. But Mrs. Camden beat her daughter to the punch by gently taking Justin's free arm and motioning him toward the recliner, which was on the other side of the living room.

"You can sit in that chair, Justin."

Mrs. Taylor nodded in agreement. "Alone."

Ruthie was mortified. She could even see Lexie snickering on her way to the couch.

To add insult to injury, Mrs. Camden motioned all the boys and girls into the living room. Then she told the boys to sit on one side of the room, and the girls on the other. Mrs. Taylor helped monitor the shocking affair.

The game was over. The ball had landed squarely in the outfielder's glove. Ruthie's reputation was toast.

ELEVEN

Kent and Lucy stood on the dance floor in a warm embrace, swaying back and forth to the familiar rhythm of a popular slow song. The two had earned the dance after spending the first hour at the front door on ID duty. So far, things were running smoothly, and the committee members had kept a close watch on alcohol consumption and behavior. Even the alumni members had been watching out for any sign of trouble.

The only thing that concerned Lucy now was the fact that the romantic dance was about to end. Couldn't it go on forever?

Kent brushed Lucy's cheek with his

lips, then whispered in her ear, "Are you wearing Angel perfume?"

Lucy nodded, and felt Kent's lips curve into a smile. "It's incredible," he said.

Lucy smiled. "So is your cologne," she returned softly, enjoying the feel of his cheek against her own.

"How did I get so lucky?" he asked, and pulled back. He looked at Lucy, smiling warmly as he took in the yellow flecks that shot through her blue eyes.

Lucy was about to tell him that *she* was the one who felt like Fortune had smiled down upon her. But before she could say anything, the slow song ended and was replaced by a loud, fast song.

Her hand dropped naturally into Kent's and they walked off the floor. Just then, Graham walked up and whispered something in Kent's ear. Kent's face whitened, and he looked at Lucy.

"Uh . . . I'll be right back, Lucy."

"Is there something wrong?"

"I . . ." He looked at Graham, who shook his head quickly and motioned him down a hallway. "I don't know." He started after Graham, then shouted over his shoulder, "I'll be right back!"

Lucy stood alone on the edge of the dance floor, confused. She followed Kent with her eyes until he disappeared around a corner.

Maybe I'll go ask the bartender if there have been any problems.

Lucy started toward the back of the room, where a bar was set up. It was packed with students holding out money, sipping beers, and shouting out drink orders.

Lucy walked behind the bar and showed the bartender her committee badge.

"How's it going back here?" she asked the tall, ponytailed man.

He looked at her and nodded with a wide grin. "We're raking it in. These kids can drink."

Kids?

"You mean twenty-one-year-old kids, right?"

He shook his head and leaned down to whisper to her. "I mean *kids*. I've never seen the money flow like this. I guess it's the first time they've been allowed to drink openly—even though it's illegal." He winked at her. "But I won't tell anyone if you won't."

Lucy's stomach turned.

She followed the bartender as he hurried down to the other side of the bar and grabbed a ten-dollar bill from a young-looking student.

"What'll it be?"

The student's face was bright with excitement. "Can you make a screwdriver?"

The bartender nodded. "I can make whatever you want, kid!"

Lucy grabbed the bartender's arm and pretended to be hip to his game. "So you're raking it in, huh? That's great!"

The guy nodded and opened the cash register's drawer, which was spilling over with cash. "I'm gonna need some more singles to break all these tens and twenties. They're even tipping with the big ones!" He pointed to the tip jar, which was filled with five- and ten-dollar bills.

Lucy leaned over, continuing the charade. "I knew they'd find a way to get wristbands. Have they told you how they did it?"

He looked at her like she was clueless. "How about asking that chick at the back door? Ten bucks and you're in like Flynn. She and some guy set it up."

Lucy's eyes zeroed in on a girl holding a box at the back door.

Rachel.

She looked at the bartender and forced a smile across her face, even though she was ready to throw up. "Thanks, man, you rock! Have a good night!"

Lucy started toward the back door, her anger building with every step. When she reached Rachel, she grabbed the young woman's arm.

"What do you think you're doing?" she demanded.

Rachel turned around, wide-eyed and innocent. "Making money for charity, what do you think?" Rachel held up the box of money. It was overflowing with five-dollar bills.

"It's *illegal*," Lucy whispered, an edge to her voice.

Rachel laughed. "Three-quarters of

the student body are under twenty-one, which means they can't drink. What I'm doing has just *quadrupled* our profits! Don't you want your darling Habitat for Humanity to have an operating budget?" Her voice had turned nasty.

"I'm going to tell Kent right now," Lucy said, spinning around. But Rachel grabbed her arm.

"He already knows."

Lucy froze, feeling her entire body go numb.

That's impossible.

Then the words of the bartender came back to her. He said Rachel had organized the sales of wristbands with a guy. What if it *was* Kent?

Rachel pounced when she saw the look of doubt cross Lucy's face. "I know you think Kent is a little angel—" Rachel's face softened, and her hand moved down Lucy's arm, where it rested gently on Lucy's hand. "Trust me. I did, too."

"What do you mean?" Lucy asked.

"It means we went out for two years, and I know that the guy he presents to the school is not the guy he really is. He's a politician, Lucy. He's not sweet, he's smooth. He can make people believe anything he wants them to, because he's an operator. He's got a gift with words. He didn't get to where he is by doing what's right."

Lucy's head felt like it was about to explode. "Why should I trust you?" she asked.

Rachel raised an eyebrow. "Because I'm the opposite of Kent. I'm a straight shooter. I tell it like it is, even if it's improper or unpopular. After all, I'm the one holding this box, aren't I? I'm not the one running around with a little eighteen-year-old date in a limousine, popping out nonalcoholic beverages, pretending to be as pure as a priest."

Lucy's mouth dropped. "How do you know about that?"

Rachel laughed. "I told him to do it! I knew the minute he offered you a real drink, you'd question him, and then you'd start digging, and then this box that I hold in my hand—and that cash till behind the bar—would be empty. I'm sorry to crash your party, but the pressure's on to raise the dough. And if you don't believe that Kent's involved, think back to the committee meeting. Whose idea was it to sell the wristbands?"

Lucy didn't want to believe it, but it was true: Kent and Graham had formulated the idea. Had they duped the entire committee while simultaneously formulating a second plan to sell underground wristbands? And what about Maya's words, which so closely matched Mrs. Camden's: *He's not perfect.*

Before Lucy could judge the truth of Rachel's awful words, her eyes settled on a sight worse than any other of the night. Tanya.

She's at the bar!

Lucy started toward the bar, but Rachel grabbed her by the arm. "Don't forget that you're on the same committee that we are. If I fall, you fall."

Lucy wanted to hit her, she was so angry. But instead, she yanked her arm away and rushed off toward Tanya. When Lucy reached her friend, she realized that Tanya had already had a beer. The cup in her hand was empty.

"What are you doing?" Lucy screeched, tugging on Tanya's arm.

Tanya looked up and started to reply, but her words came out all wrong. She was stuttering. "I—I just, uh, just had a drink," she barely managed to say.

A sickening thought struck Lucy.

Is she drunk?

"I—I was nervous," Tanya said. "I needed . . . I needed to relax. Aaron—"

Lucy looked around. Where *was* Aaron? Why wasn't he watching her? "Aaron what?"

Just then, Tanya's eyes began to droop. "I—I feel really sleepy."

Lucy grabbed Tanya around the waist and helped lift her off the stool. "We're going home," she said. "I'm putting you to bed. You're drunk and you're sick—and I can't believe this is happening!"

Just then, Aaron walked up. He saw Lucy helping Tanya to walk.

"Is she okay?" he asked, confused.

Lucy shot him a nasty look. "Just help me get her to the limo."

As they started for the front door, Lucy saw Kent walking up to the stage with a microphone in hand. She threw him an even nastier look. His face turned white, just as it had when Graham had pulled him away, and Lucy knew, at that moment, that he was guilty.

She and Aaron pulled Tanya to the limo and the chauffeur ran around and opened the door. When they got Tanya inside, her head dropped to the seat and her body went limp. She had passed out.

Meanwhile, back in the dance hall, the music stopped and Kent's voice filled the room. He announced that minors had been caught drinking and the bar was being shut down. As the crowd of students booed and hissed, Kent left the stage and ran out after Lucy. But by the time he reached the parking lot, the limo was gone.

Back at the Camdens', Ruthie was throwing a tantrum. Standing in the kitchen, she controlled her voice so that her peers couldn't hear her but she shouted loudly with every arm, leg, and baby-blue toenail that God had given her.

"How can I have a cool party if the boys can't sit next to the girls? I'm not a baby anymore! This is worse than not having a party at all! This is *punishment*!"

Simon walked into the kitchen like Superman and diplomatically made a heroic proposition to his mother. "Why don't you let them sit next to whoever they want, and *I'll* sit in the recliner? I'll make sure nothing happens."

Ruthie saw a tiny speck of light at the end of her long tunnel. She looked at her mother, who was mulling the thought over.

Simon put his arms around his mother's shoulders and gave her a big squeeze. "Come on, Mom. You can trust me."

Mrs. Camden looked at Simon, who was grinning. How could she say no to that smile? She threw up her hands in surrender.

"Why not?"

Ruthie's luck had taken an upward turn. Having Simon in the room was *even better* than having no one.

All the girls think Simon's a hottie, and boys think he's cool.

Simon draped his arm around

Ruthie's shoulder and escorted his tortured sister back into the living room. Ruthie thought she would burst, she was so proud to be next to him.

When they entered the room, all the kids looked up at Simon, impressed at the mere sight of the imposing tenth grader. He was one cool dude. Then they looked at his arm, so casually embracing his little sister.

Ruthie was cool again.

And she knew it.

"Scoot over," she directed Lexie.

For once, Lexie followed orders. Then Ruthie's eyes moved to Justin. She pointed to him and then to the empty seat beside her.

Justin stood up and the room filled with whistles and catcalls as he made his way to the couch. Which, of course, prompted Mrs. Camden to peek her head into the room. Simon glared at her and she scurried back to the kitchen.

As Ruthie grabbed the remote control and pressed the play button, she prayed her brother wouldn't rat her out. . . .

TWELVE

Thirty seconds into Lexie's movie, the
Motion Picture Association of America
rating popped up like a three-headed
monster. The gigantic letter R bared its
psychological fangs at Ruthie. Simon
shot his little sister a look and was
surprised to find that Ruthie wasn't
watching the screen—she was watching
him.

It's not dirty, she mouthed to him.

Simon's brow furrowed.

Is it violent? he mouthed back.

Ruthie shook her head, but Simon
squirmed in his seat. If an R-rated movie
wasn't dirty and it wasn't violent, then
what was it?

Simon crossed his arms and decided that his little sister had suffered enough over the course of planning the party. He would let the rating slide so long as nothing questionable lit up the TV screen.

But ten minutes into the film, a man and woman embraced in a long, romantic kiss.

Simon shot Ruthie another look and, once again, found that Ruthie was staring at him. She shrugged innocently, then looked at the movie screen as though there was nothing wrong.

That little rascal. She's done it again. She's manipulated me into feeling sorry for her.

But just as Simon was about to suggest watching a different movie, Ruthie threw him a desperate look. One that begged for mercy in a time of great trial and tribulation.

Simon closed his eyes and sat back in his seat. He tried to get comfortable, and reminded himself of the time he had thrown a party. He had brought his girlfriend Deena over, and his mother had asked her where she got the pretty ring that adorned her wedding finger. When Deena answered that it was from Simon, Mrs. Camden took the ring off Deena's finger and said, "When the two of you decide to get engaged, you can have the ring back. Until then, Simon should limit himself to chocolates."

The worst thing of all was that Mrs. Camden had done it at the party, in front of all of Simon's friends. It was horrible, an event that took him half a school year to live down.

No, he wouldn't bust Ruthie unless the movie got racy. After all, what was wrong with a little romance?

But two minutes later, the romance was racing ahead full throttle, and Simon foresaw an ugly crash with Mrs. Camden intervening. Where was the remote control? He definitely needed to fast-forward through some of this.

Suddenly Simon realized that none of the kids were watching the TV screen, but rather were shifting uncomfortably in their seats. Some were staring down at their hands; others were pulling at threads in their jeans or picking at their fingernails. A few of the braver souls were exchanging looks with one another.

They're more uncomfortable than I am!

Just as Simon was about to stand and announce the end of the movie, Justin Taylor beat him to it. The lanky kid pulled his baseball cap down low over his eyes and asked if anyone wanted to go in the backyard and play basketball.

Within milliseconds, the entire party was *racing* for the back door—and Ruthie, afraid of Simon's wrath, took the lead.

Tanya wasn't breathing.

Lucy was panicking.

She looked at the chauffeur and screamed, "Get her to the hospital!"

But the chauffeur was already driving as fast as he could. Across from Lucy, Aaron was praying.

When Lucy saw Aaron's closed eyes, she couldn't stop herself from yelling. "You better be praying! This is your fault! She was your date, and you didn't even watch out for her!"

But inside, Lucy knew it was as much her fault as anyone's. She had voted to sell the alcohol, even when something deep inside her had been uncomfortable with the idea. She had wanted so desperately to be liked, and to not cause waves among the upperclassmen, that she had ignored her own sense of right and wrong.

Then again, she really had believed that the safeguards they had established would work. She thought they were fail-safe. How had it gone so wrong?

She looked down at Tanya's head in her lap, terrified to think of what might happen to her. She didn't even know CPR. Why hadn't she taken that class that was offered?

Why, why, why?

The limousine screeched up to the ER entrance of the hospital, and the chauffeur ran around to open the door. But before he could get it open, a group of emergency medical technicians beat him to it.

"She's not breathing!" Lucy screamed as the EMTs climbed inside.

A woman took Lucy's hand to calm her while the others surrounded Tanya's limp body. "Did she take any drugs?"

Lucy shook her head, "I don't think so, but . . ."

The woman nodded, trying to calm Lucy down. "But what?"

"She drank."

"Beer?"

Lucy looked at Aaron. Aaron shrugged helplessly. "I don't know, I didn't see. She kept leaving me. She kept running off!" he exclaimed.

Lucy tried to gather her thoughts. She took a deep breath as the other EMTs strapped Tanya onto a gurney, administering life support as they wheeled her off.

"She was drinking alcohol, but I don't know how much," Lucy cried. "She was stuttering, and then she said she was sleepy. We started walking her to the limo—I wanted to take her home—and then she passed out. Suddenly . . ." Lucy started to cry. "She stopped breathing."

Lucy's tears were coming fast and hard. The woman gave her a quick hug, then promised that they'd do everything in their power to save Tanya. She ran into the hospital, leaving Lucy and Aaron alone in the back of the limousine.

When Lucy looked at Aaron, her anger melted into more tears. He put his arms around her, then pulled her out of the limo and into the hospital as the kind chauffeur followed them in

What if Tanya didn't make it?

THIRTEEN

As Lucy waited for news on Tanya, Ruthie was in a circle of girls fighting with Lexie; meanwhile, the boys played basketball.

"Why did you pick such a dirty movie?" Ruthie demanded. A few of the girls nodded in agreement, staring Lexie down in an impressive display of group power.

Lexie tossed her charcoal hair behind her. It was a gesture every girl in Ruthie's academy knew well. It meant Lexie was ready to engage in all-out war. "I didn't know it was so dirty," she spat. "Was I supposed to preview it before bringing it into the wholesome Camden household?"

Some of the girls laughed, stepping away from Ruthie. "Yeah," a girl named Jessie said with a sweep of her arm. "My mother almost made me wear a jacket over my tank top because she thought Mrs. Camden would send me home!"

Ruthie leaped at the girl, but her two remaining friends grabbed her, knowing that a fistfight would be the end of the party.

Ruthie looked at the basketball court and was horrified to see that all the boys had stopped playing and were staring at the girls.

Before Ruthie could regroup, Lexie motioned to her clique of girls. "Let's blow this Popsicle stand. Party's at *my* pad."

Jessie nodded and followed. Then all of the other girls, except for Lily, fell in line. Just as the group was about to leave the backyard, Lexie turned around.

"And by the way, Simon isn't as cool as you think. His Nikes are *so* 2000."

For once, Ruthie was speechless. How had her new best friend suddenly become her enemy?

As the boys resumed their game of

basketball, Ruthie turned to Lily, glad to have at least one friend left. But Lily rolled her eyes. "Why are you hanging out with her anyway?"

Ruthie shrugged.

Why am *I hanging out with her?*

"She makes you act like she does," Lily said. "Ick." Lily started to walk back inside, but Ruthie stopped her.

"Wait."

Lily turned around.

"You're right. I act like a jerk when I'm with her. I even helped her spread the news that your rabbits were out of style. I'm sorry."

Lily shrugged and walked back to her friend. "That's okay. Even *I'm* getting sick of them. I mean, how many times can you marvel at bunnies giving birth? Pretty soon you run out of backyard space."

Ruthie tried to smile as she sat down at the picnic table. But she couldn't. She wished she had never had the party at all. Even Justin thought she was a loser. Could she possibly be more humiliated than she was at this moment?

Suddenly a shout reverberated from deep within the Camden house. The shout was so loud that lights went on all the way up and down the quiet Glenoak street. Its particular timbre struck terror into Ruthie's heart. It originated from the breast of none other than Mrs. Camden.

"Ruthie Camden! Get in here right now!"

Ruthie closed her eyes in surrender. She was dead meat; she had forgotten to eject the tape.

Mrs. Camden stood in the kitchen with the dirty videotape in one hand and the G-rated movie in the other.

"I didn't do that!" Ruthie exclaimed, then crossed her arms defiantly as if to second her claim of innocence. "The video store mixed them up! I was as shocked as you are!"

Annie's stance was unflinching. She pointed to the table, her argument so strong she didn't even need to speak.

Sitting on the kitchen table was Lexie's bag. Its contents were strewn across the tabletop, the R-rated case exposed like a piece of evidence in a criminal court case.

"Do you think I'm stupid?" Mrs. Camden finally demanded.

Ruthie considered pleading the Fifth, but silence was impossible for her in the heat of battle. "How did you get through the trophies?"

"What trophies?"

"Under the bed!"

Mrs. Camden had no idea what Ruthie was talking about, nor did she care. "The bag was right here, on the table, open wide for everyone to see."

Ruthie's eyes flared with anger.

Lexie. That conniving, little . . .

But Mrs. Camden was spitting fire. In fact, her hands hadn't stopped flailing since the moment Ruthie had walked through the back door—where, unbeknownst to both of them, all the boys from the party were peering in.

"You weren't even smart enough to turn off the TV when you went outside!" Mrs. Camden said in amazement. "That's what really surprises me. That you, Ruthie Camden, failed to cover such obvious tracks."

"We went outside *because* it was so dirty," she argued. "I should get credit for that! I didn't *know* it was so dirty or I would have *never* put it in!"

"It's rated *R*, Ruthie. You know how to read."

Ruthie shrank back in feigned shock at her mother's accusations. "*Lexie* brought it."

Mrs. Camden sighed, wishing that her daughter had just admitted her guilt. The punishment would be much easier. But all the deceit, that was the thing that always got Ruthie into trouble.

"Do you and Lexie share a brain?" Mrs. Camden asked. She stared wide-eyed at her daughter, waiting to see what sort of creative response the girl could concoct. She was surprised when Ruthie merely shook her head. Mrs. Camden continued.

"Sometimes you're quite a nice girl, Ruthie, but other times you're downright manipulative. This is one of those times, and your party is over—with more social pain to follow. Now get upstairs."

As Ruthie started up the stairs, she saw all the boys in the backyard scatter off to the basketball court. They had heard everything. She looked down into the living room to see if Lily had witnessed her humiliation. Luckily, Lily waved and blew her friend a supportive kiss.

Just then, Simon started down the stairs. When he passed Ruthie, he attempted to hide his smile—a smile that wasn't mean or provoking, but rather a smile that came from a place of shared pain. He'd been the victim of Mrs. Camden's motherly wrath on more than one occasion.

Unfortunately, Ruthie didn't interpret the smile this way. As soon as she saw the corners of his mouth curled ever so slightly upward, she shouted, "Shut up!"

At the same moment, the telephone rang and Mrs. Camden reached for it. She looked up at Simon, who was smiling even wider from his little sister's verbal whipping.

"You heard her," Mrs. Camden said, annoyed that her son was grinning in the midst of such a frustrating battle.

"Hello?" Mrs. Camden said, failing to mask the exhaustion in her voice.

Simon started to laugh at the whole scenario.

It's nice to be a sophomore.

But when he saw his mother's face,

the laughter faded. She was white as a ghost.

"What's wrong?" he asked as his mother hung up the phone.

She turned and grabbed her son's hand. "It's Lucy. She's at the hospital. Her friend Tanya is in a coma."

FOURTEEN

The next morning, Lucy woke up in her own bed at the Camden house. She'd spent the entire night at the hospital, pacing back and forth in the hallway, waiting for news on Tanya's condition. According to the doctors, Tanya had alcohol poisoning—a condition caused by the rapid consumption of too much alcohol.

This news had shocked Lucy. How was it possible that Tanya had drunk so much in so little time? And why hadn't Aaron kept an eye on her? Or maybe a better question was: why hadn't Lucy kept an eye on her? Lucy was racked with guilt.

I knew how nervous she was. I was so

engrossed in my date that I didn't even pay attention to her.

When Kent had arrived at the hospital, Lucy forced herself to control her temper. She didn't want to have a confrontation in the middle of such a traumatic situation—after all, Tanya's family would be arriving at any moment. She wanted to be there to support them, not to create more drama. So instead, Lucy told Kent she wasn't in the mood for talking and quietly walked away. She was glad that he hadn't forced the issue.

When Mrs. Camden had arrived, Lucy collapsed into her mother's arms. She spent the rest of the night there, like a child again, praying that Tanya would be all right. But when morning came, there was still no news and Mrs. Camden had convinced Lucy to come back to the house.

Now Lucy lay in her own bed at home, looking blankly at the walls of the room she and her sister Mary had once shared. She wished she could turn back the clock. There were so many things she would change. All the fights she and Mary had once had. Or the drive she had let her friend Jennifer go on with Jennifer's wild sister. That drive had ended in an awful car crash, and Lucy's friend had died.

Would yet another poor decision on Lucy's part end in the same way?

Lucy closed her eyes and prayed. But before she could finish the prayer, the telephone rang. Lucy reached over and picked it up, hoping that her prayer had just been answered.

"Hello?" Lucy asked hopefully.

A voice Lucy had never heard before was on the other line. "Good morning. This is Susan Biggs from the office of the university president."

Lucy felt terror creeping up in her throat. The president of the university? Why would President O'Hare's office be calling Lucy?

"Yes?" Lucy asked, concerned that the call had to do with Tanya. News must have spread quickly.

"I'm looking for Lucy Camden. She wasn't in her dorm room and we thought that perhaps she had spent the night at her permanent address?"

Lucy took a deep breath, knowing

that she had to face the music once and for all. "I'm Lucy," she said.

The woman's voice betrayed no emotion whatsoever. "The president would like to speak with you at ten A.M."

Lucy looked at the clock. It was nine-twenty-five.

"Uh . . . this morning?" she managed to say.

"That's correct," the woman confirmed. "So we'll see you in half an hour."

Lucy realized that she had no choice in the matter. She thanked the woman and hung up the phone. Then she climbed out of bed and looked in her old closet. She didn't have much to choose from, as she had taken all of her nice clothes with her to college.

When she looked in the mirror, she didn't even care that her hair was as wild as it had been on the day of her trek to the cafeteria. Somehow it didn't matter anymore. None of those stupid, petty concerns mattered. Tanya was in the hospital, and Lucy would never be the same again.

*　　*　　*

Half an hour later, Lucy stood outside a
tall, heavy wooden door with a gold plate
that read: GENEVIEVE O'HARE, PRESIDENT.

Lucy breathed in deeply, attempting
to center herself before entering. She
opened the door. Inside, the president's
assistant, Susan, who had a blond bun on
the top of her head, sat at a large desk.
When the woman looked up, she
addressed Lucy with an air of formality.

"Lucy Camden?"

Lucy nodded. "Yes, ma'am."

The woman pointed to another wooden
door. "They're waiting for you."

They?

Lucy forced herself to smile and
reached for the door, swallowing hard.
When she opened it, she was surprised to
see that the office was full of people. People she knew.

Kent looked up and then looked away.
Somebody's got a guilt complex.

Lucy's eyes quickly perused the rest of
the room. Rachel sat in a chair against a
wall. Graham was standing by the door.
Aaron was sitting on the floor. All the
other committee members and officers
filled the room as well. And even an adult

Lucy had once seen at a panel lecture, Mr. Lemmons, the student government sponsor, was there.

In the back of the room, facing the door and seated at a large oak desk, was the president of the university, a powerful-looking African American woman with gentle eyes but a deep, commanding voice. President O'Hare motioned Lucy inside.

When the door shut behind her, the president stood up. She walked around to the front of her desk and sat down upon it, an action which immediately put the students more at ease.

"You all know why you're here," President O'Hare began. "An underage student was served alcohol at a school-sponsored event and is now in a coma from alcohol poisoning. And those of you in this room, in a certain way, were responsible for it. I'd really like to believe that you were wise enough and prudent enough to have established some safety precautions. After all, you're given a great deal of responsibility by this university. A responsibility that, when ignored, can affect the lives of our students in dramatic ways. So before I jump to any conclusions, and before I begin dealing out the proper punishments, I need you to tell me how something like this could happen."

President O'Hare looked around the room, waiting for someone to respond. But all of the students were speechless. Finally, Kent raised his hand, and Lucy was very curious to see what he had to say. Maybe he would do the right thing and admit his blame in the selling of wristbands.

"Yes, Kent?"

He took a deep breath.

"I'm not sure where to begin. I feel awful about everything that has happened, and I spent the entire night worrying, wondering what my role in all of this has been, wondering how responsible for this trauma I am. . . ."

Lucy watched Kent's face, which was solemn and earnest. Was it all a show?

"And I guess there's a part of me that feels like I've failed as a president, that I've failed the student government, failed the school. . . ."

He looked around at the people standing in the room, carefully meeting each of their eyes. When he settled on Lucy, she almost looked away. But the sincerity in his eyes was impossible to deny.

"But then there's another part of me that knows how seriously I considered the issue. I worked really hard coming up with a plan that I thought was foolproof."

He looked at Graham quickly and then looked away. Lucy felt her blood rise. Kent was going to lie about the whole thing! And he was looking at Graham to make sure he was with him on the story!

Lucy looked at Rachel, who sat in the chair with her arms crossed, staring daggers at Kent.

I bet he scapegoats Rachel!

As Kent continued explaining the wristband solution that he and Graham had come up with, Lucy was getting angrier by the minute—especially when she realized that the president believed every word Kent had said.

President O'Hare stood up.

"I know that alcohol has been sold in the past at school functions, so it's not as though you were acting out of line by considering such a thing. Maybe this is a policy that we need to rethink for the future. But what worries me right now is how easily your ID plan was sabotaged. I want to know how it happened and who, if anybody, was responsible for it."

Lucy looked around the room and discovered that everyone else was doing the same thing. Although, by and large, all eyes were settling on Rachel.

Kent raised his hand again. "Maybe there are certain people in this room who need to think about resigning."

He looked at Rachel, whose face was made of stone.

Kent continued. "Maybe we all need to go home and think seriously about our blame in the situation. If a resignation is in order, perhaps we can inform you of our decision by tomorrow?"

The president nodded, agreeing with his plan. But Lucy wanted to shout, *Maybe* you *need to think about resigning!*

Lucy suppressed her anger and forced herself to think about the really important matter. The matter of Tanya. She raised her hand and the president nodded.

"I understand that you have to address all of these concerns," Lucy said, looking President O'Hare in the eye. "And

I understand that we as a group have to address these concerns, but . . ."

Lucy felt a knot well up in her throat. She took a moment to breathe, attempting to keep her voice from shaking. She didn't want to cry right now. She wanted to be strong. "But what about Tanya?" she finally said. "Nobody's talking about *Tanya*. She's my friend." Lucy looked at President O'Hare, who nodded. "She's somebody's daughter, someone's sister. And she could *die*." Lucy looked right at Kent.

"The least this group can do for the pain it's caused is donate some of the money we earned to Tanya's family. Her medical bills alone will be in the thousands. And we could send a bouquet of flowers, we can visit her, and pray for her, and *feel* what could be lost if she dies."

President O'Hare walked over to Lucy and squeezed her hand. "I think that's a great idea," she said.

Meanwhile, at Ruthie's academy, the spunky fifth grader was attempting to rebound from her Valentine's Day mishap. And just to spite Lexie, she had painted all ten of her toenails in different colors. Not a single shade matched. And it was a smash hit.

But before she could make too many reparations to her reputation, she had to finish the final round of her mother's social punishment: Ruthie had to hand out written apologies to all the guests who had come to her party. And as proof that she had accomplished the task, she had to ask everybody to take their notes home and have them signed by their parents.

Cruel punishment indeed.

She had saved the most horrific delivery for the last hour of the school day. The delivery to Justin Taylor.

As soon as the school bell rang and the kids poured out of their classrooms, Ruthie ran out onto the school grounds, scanning the grassy expanse for a sign of the boy in the L.A. Dodgers cap.

But right at the moment when she thought she spotted him, she felt a tap on her left shoulder. She turned to her left, but nobody was there. Then she spun around to her right, wondering who had succeeded in tricking her.

To her surprise, Justin stood behind her with a shy grin on his face, his hands buried deep in his jean pockets. "Hey," he said softly.

Ruthie felt her feisty demeanor soften. Suddenly nervous, she dropped her hands, which were positioned powerfully on her hips, to her side. "Hey," she replied.

Justin shifted uncomfortably on his feet. "I just wanted to say I'm sorry that Lexie ruined your party."

Ruthie felt her cheeks redden. "It was my own fault," she said. "I shouldn't have let her bring that stupid movie."

Justin laughed. "Yeah, it was pretty embarrassing."

Suddenly Ruthie remembered the note and she handed it to him. But before he read it, he looked at her. He had something else to say.

"I wanted to tell you that your mom's not so bad. At least not compared to mine. My mom actually wanted to stay with me at your party. She wanted to sit in the chair beside me. Thank God my dad stepped in, or I would have been the biggest loser in the whole school."

Ruthie snickered. "Yeah, that *is* pretty bad!"

Justin looked down at the letter and smiled. "She'll be more than happy to sign this. She'll probably call your mom and congratulate her on a job well done."

The two kids laughed and then Justin looked at the ground. He seemed nervous and shy again.

"Hey," he began, and kicked at the tip of a rock in the ground. "Do you want to go see a matinee sometime? You know, a PG movie?"

Ruthie shrugged. "My mom won't let me go on a date alone."

Justin looked at Ruthie like she was a curious insect that had just landed before him. "*Hello*. Neither will mine. My mom and dad will be sitting right beside us."

If Ruthie had been chewing a big wad of bubble gum, she would have spit it out she laughed so hard. "That's *so lame*!"

But the truth was, it made Ruthie happy to know that there was somebody else out there who had a family like hers. Maybe it wasn't so square to be square after all.

FIFTEEN

The next day, after Rachel and Graham had resigned from ASG, the Camden family sat around their table, praying for Tanya before beginning their meal. When the prayer was over, Lucy turned to her mother and confessed something.

"You know how defensive I got when you disagreed with me about selling alcohol at the dance?"

Mrs. Camden nodded.

"Well, I was defensive because I knew you were right. Down deep, I never agreed with the decision we made. But I went along with the group anyway because I was afraid of being ostracized. I should have trusted my feelings. I should have been true to myself and my beliefs. I thought I learned that lesson in high school, but it looks like I'm learning it all over again."

Mrs. Camden reached across the table and put her hand on her daughter's hands. Lucy felt tears welling up in her eyes again. She looked at her father.

"And when you said that everyone needed to leave me alone because I had made my own decision, those words terrified me—because you were right: it was *my* decision. And look at the results. . . ."

Suddenly the tears she was holding back came flooding out. The reverend stood up and walked to his daughter's side. He put his arms around her and kissed her gently on the forehead. "If you knew how many mistakes I've made in my life, you'd be a little easier on yourself," he said. "We all mess up. The important thing is that you've owned up to everything, which is braver than most people would be. I'm proud of you, Lucy."

Just as the rest of the family began murmuring words of love and support, there was a knock at the front door. Lucy jumped. What if it was someone coming to deliver news from the hospital?

"I'll get it," she said, and started for the door.

When she opened it, she was surprised to find Kent standing outside. He quickly held up his hand, making her promise to let him speak. "I know you're mad at me. I don't know the reason, but I know that you are. And whatever it is that I did, I'm sorry."

Lucy looked at him, both eyebrows raised in disbelief. "You don't know what you did?"

"No," Kent said. "And I think we should talk about it."

"Fine," Lucy said, starting out the door. "Let's talk right now."

But Kent shook his head. "Not yet. I have some big news for you. Can I come in?"

Lucy stumbled for a minute, not sure of how to react. She finally opened the door. He walked in and saw the family sitting at the table. He smiled at them all. "Hi, I'm Kent. I'm sorry to interrupt your dinner."

He was greeted with silence from the group. Finally, the reverend stood up and held out his hand warmly.

"Sorry to be rude, I'm Lucy's father, Reverend Camden." He pulled out a chair and looked at his family, his eyes requesting that they all be kind to the young man, regardless of what he had done. "Sit down, please."

Kent shook his head. "Thank you, but I just wanted to deliver some great news. I just got back from the hospital. Tanya has come out of the coma. She's going to be okay!"

The entire family ecstatically jumped up out of their seats. Before they had time to ask for details, Lucy had already grabbed the keys to the family van and was headed out the front door.

Lucy walked into the hospital room with a large bouquet of flowers. Tanya, who was lying down, immediately perked up at the sight of her closest college friend.

"Lucy!" Tanya exclaimed.

"I'm so happy!" Lucy squealed, then saw all the other bouquets that filled the room. Tanya's room looked like a flower shop. Clearly, all the ASG officers and committee members had taken Lucy up on her request. "Where can I put these?"

Tanya shrugged and motioned to the bed, the only remaining plot of empty space. "Right there."

Lucy laid the bouquet at Tanya's foot, then leaned over and gave Tanya the biggest squeeze ever. When the two girls finally let go of one another, Lucy raised her hands as though preparing to give a well-rehearsed speech.

"First and foremost," she said, "I want to apologize for ever going along with the committee on the ball's alcohol policy. I knew it was wrong and I voted yes anyway—"

But before Lucy could get another word out, Tanya interrupted her. She spoke with a frustration and passion that Lucy had never witnessed in her before.

"I wish everyone would stop blaming the school, and its officers, and the committee, and themselves. . . . I wish people would just stop blaming, period."

Lucy shook her head. "You're wrong, Tanya. We *are* at fault. We had the responsibility of making sure that nothing went wrong. And something did go wrong."

Tanya sighed. "Listen, Lucy. In a certain sense, you may be right. But *I'm* the one who chose to drink. My fate is my own fault. I'm not a child anymore."

"No, but you're still a teenager."

"So are you," Tanya retorted. "Did *you* choose to drink?"

Lucy scoffed. "No, but I didn't have a date who was pressuring me."

"Neither did I."

Lucy started to protest further, wanting to heap more blame on Aaron— or anyone for that matter. She struggled to find another scapegoat. "I didn't have a date who made me nervous," she managed.

"Aaron didn't make me nervous either. It was the situation, Lucy. I'm not a gregarious person like you. I don't do well when I'm with people I don't know. I always feel like I don't fit in. And so I made a stupid choice. I chose to drink because I thought it would help me relax. And Aaron . . ."

Tanya sighed. "*I* should be apologiz-

ing to *him*. Every time he asked me to
dance, I said I had to go to the bathroom.
But instead of going to the bathroom, I
would sneak off to have a drink. I really
believed it would help me have a good
time. But it didn't."

Suddenly Lucy felt awful. She had
thrown Aaron more dirty looks and com-
ments than she'd ever thrown anyone in
her life. And for no justifiable reason.

Just then, Aaron, who had been
standing outside the doorway, walked in
with a bouquet of flowers. He had overheard the tail end of the conversation.

"Lucy's right," he said. "I should have
never let you start drinking. You were my
date, and I knew you were nervous. I
should have been more careful; I should
have made you feel more comfortable. . . ."

Tanya groaned. "It's not your fault! It
was nobody's fault but my own. I made a
bad choice that I'll never make again."
Tanya looked around the room at all the
bouquets. "The only problem I have now
is finding a place to put all these flowers.
I never knew I had so many friends."

Lucy reached out and hugged Tanya

again. "You do." Then Lucy looked at Aaron, realizing that she had been completely wrong in blaming him. She couldn't believe she had let herself jump to conclusions so quickly. "I'm sorry I blamed you, Aaron. . . ."

He smiled and shook his head. "I understand. When something like this happens, we all need someplace to put our anger."

Aaron bit his lip then, as though he was thinking of saying something more to Lucy, but wasn't sure if it was appropriate. "Speaking of which . . . ," he said tentatively, and set the bouquet on the foot of the bed. He sat down and looked Lucy in the eye.

"I hope you don't mind me butting into your business, but I know you're angry at Kent, and I know you think he organized the wristband sales. But he didn't."

Lucy felt her face go pale. Was it possible that she had misjudged the situation so completely? That she had misjudged not only Aaron, but Kent, too?

"How do you know?" she asked.

"Because I overheard Graham talking

to Kent in one of the hallways at the dance. I was out looking for Tanya, and I heard Graham admit to Kent that he and Rachel had decided to sell a few wristbands, but that the sales had gotten out of hand. He apologized, but Kent wouldn't hear it. He got really angry and said that he was shutting the bar down immediately, and that if anything bad happened, Graham and Rachel had better own up to it. That was when I walked around the corner and spotted you and Tanya at the bar."

Lucy put her hand over her mouth, she was so upset at herself. How could she have jumped to so many conclusions? Maybe God was trying to teach her a serious lesson. She closed her eyes, praying for an idea on how to remedy the situation.

But was there a remedy? If the situation were reversed, and Kent had judged her guilty without the slightest bit of evidence, would she be able to forgive him? What would he have to do to erase the bitterness that most certainly would gnaw in the pit of her stomach?

For one, he'd have to be sincere. Lucy

nodded to herself: she had that criterion down. But she knew it would take more than sincerity to rid the situation of awkwardness. It would take comedy. After all, she thought, laughter was the greatest medicine of all. But how could she make him laugh after all that had happened?

And then it occurred to her.

"It's perfect!" she said out loud, ignoring the confused glances that Aaron and Tanya threw her way. She stood up, mentally scribbling the list of items necessary to pull off the shenanigan. She would need a big strip of cardboard. And maybe her baby brothers' silver Slinky. What else?

Lucy grabbed her keys, kissed her two friends' cheeks, and ran out of the room without an explanation of any kind. Her mind was spinning. She had to work fast—the day was almost over. . . .

SIXTEEN

At six-thirty P.M., just as the sun was dropping beneath the horizon, Lucy walked across campus to the senior dormitories. She held a rectangular-shaped piece of cardboard in her arms and a small velvet bag with a golden drawstring. She walked with purpose toward the A wing, where Kent resided.

She spotted his window up on the third floor and sneaked behind a bush directly below it. She waited there until the sun had dropped far enough below the earth that the bright orange streaks across the sky were replaced by twilight's soft purple and grays.

When the first star of the night

appeared just inches from the crescent moon, she stepped out onto the sidewalk.

She opened up her velvet bag and smiled. The bag was donated by Ruthie, who had seen the one big hole in her big sister's plan: how would Lucy find enough rocks on campus to hit a window clear up on the third floor?

Lucy dug into the bag and pulled out a tiny green marble. She kissed it, took aim at the window, and let it fly.

It missed Kent's window by ten feet.

This is why you left the sports to Mary.

Lucy retrieved another marble and studied the window. She bit her lip hard, concentrating. She extended her arm, practicing the motion of a baseball throw. Why hadn't she taken those pitching lessons Matt and Mary had offered her so long ago?

The next marble sailed upward, upward, upward . . . and nailed a window on the fourth floor. Suddenly a blond head appeared in the window. The guy who owned the overgrown mane of gold threw the window open and shouted down to her.

"You looking for me?" he asked hopefully.

Lucy turned red. "Uh . . . no. I'm trying to hit Kent's window."

The guy nodded, grabbed a camera tripod, extended its legs, tipped it over, and bent out the window.

"Uh . . . ," Lucy began. "You don't have to do that."

The guy dipped the tripod carefully downward. "I saw you throw," he said. "Without me, you'll be pinging my window all night."

Lucy put her bag of marbles on the ground. He was probably right. Then she grabbed her cardboard rectangle, which had small holes punched all the way down the left margins. Through the holes, Lucy had coiled Sam and David's silver Slinky. In essence, she was holding a gigantic notebook.

Just then, Kent's head appeared in the window. He spotted the camera tripod and, confused, opened his screen. He leaned out and looked up at the curly-headed blond guy.

"What's up, man?"

The guy shook his head. "I don't know, ask her." He pointed down at Lucy, who was now holding up the oversized notebook.

Kent couldn't help but smile when he saw the words she had scribbled across it in bright red marker:

Forgive me?

Kent reached in and grabbed a notebook off his desk.

He scribbled one letter on the first page and held it up:

O

Then a second letter on the second page:

K

Lucy felt relief sweep over her as Kent leaned into his room again and fumbled around in his desk. But she was still worried: What if he forgave her but didn't want to see her anymore? What if she had crossed a line with him, and he decided he only wanted to be friends? It could be hard to date a person who had mistrusted you.

Lucy watched Kent retrieve a tiny box from his desk. He turned it upside down and she saw a tiny assortment of pastel items fall out of the box into his hand. He sorted through the contents, picking each up individually, looking it over, and placing it aside as if it didn't suit his purpose. Finally, he grabbed hold of something pink and tiny. He smiled. This was the one.

He leaned out and tossed the mysterious item toward Lucy. She reached up, determined to catch whatever prize it was he had thrown. Just as her hands were about to encircle the gift, Lucy lost her balance slightly and wobbled. The pink trinket grazed her palm and bounced off into the grass.

"Ah!" Lucy exclaimed. She went running after it, then dropped to her knees, combing the lawn for any speckle of pink. At last, she saw it and reached out, her small fingers gingerly picking it up from the grass. It was a pink candy heart with two words printed across it:

Be Mine

Before Lucy could stand up and accept the offer, the curly-headed guy shouted out in exasperation, "Get down there and kiss her already!"

At which point, Kent turned and ran out the door, down the steps, through the exit, and into the arms of Lucy—which he covered with kisses before settling, finally, on her soft and waiting lips.

DON'T MISS THIS BRAND-NEW, ORIGINAL 7TH HEAVEN STORY

Coming June 2002!

DUDE
RANCH

The Camdens are on vacation in the Arizona outback! Well, sort of. They've agreed to help a ranching family convert a failing ranch into a profitable "dude" ranch—so they'll have to feed horses, drive cattle, fix buildings, and even dough-punch . . . whatever *that* means! But not all the members of the ranching family appreciate the Camdens' help. Lucy wants to get closer to handsome, brooding Luke, who resents anything smelling of charity. Meanwhile, Simon and Ruthie are off to find a hidden treasure!

DON'T MISS THIS BRAND-NEW,
ORIGINAL 7TH HEAVEN STORY

Now Available!

CAMP
CAMDEN

Lucy and Ruthie are off to summer camp in sunny Malibu, California, where swimming, boating, and horseback riding aren't their only pastimes! Lucy's teaching a class that catches the attention of a handsome counselor, and Ruthie is pulling pranks that make everyone take notice! Meanwhile, back at the Camden house, Simon's trying his latest money-making scheme—day-trading on the Internet! But is the stock market ready for Simon Camden?

DON'T MISS THIS BRAND-NEW,
HEARTWARMING COLLECTION OF
ORIGINAL 7TH HEAVEN STORIES

Now Available!

LUCY'S
ANGEL

While visiting her grandfather in Arizona, Lucy Camden uncovers a beautiful angel ornament in his basement—one that seems to have a magical message. Meanwhile, flying home from Buffalo proves disastrous for Mary. When an unexpected blizzard forces her to camp out on the floor of an airport terminal, she wonders what could be worse. Then Matt picks up a stranded motorist on his way to a swingin' new year in Las Vegas. But the trouble is that this impersonator thinks he's actually *Elvis*!

13th